The American Guerillas

The American Guerillas

Rod MacDonald

ARCHWAY
PUBLISHING

Archway Publishing books may be ordered through booksellers or by contacting:

Archway Publishing
1663 Liberty Drive
Bloomington, IN 47403
www.archwaypublishing.com
844-669-3957

ISBN: 978-1-6657-0373-4 (sc)
ISBN: 978-1-6657-0374-1 (e)

Library of Congress Control Number: 2021904125

Print information available on the last page.

Archway Publishing rev. date: 4/8/2021

For Brian

Editor's Note

The American Guerillas is the masterpiece of Rod MacDonald's literary work, and rivals his most provocative and entertaining original songs.

This is also the second of who-knows-how-many literary projects that Rod and I have worked on together. Here I want to pay tribute to the enjoyment, engagement, and good home cooking that Rod and his family have given me so many times over the past ten to fifteen years. It was in a dinner conversation that Rod made brief mention of his "archives," where he had stored thirty to forty years of prose and fiction.

At the time, I had been researching how America's oral traditions, music, and public intellectuals had created an honest engagement during the post–World War II, anti-Communist era, irrationally sold as "protection" of American democracy. We survived, producing the urban folk, bebop jazz, jazz-influenced rural music known as bluegrass, the Beat poets and performers, and strengthened the America epic.

I also spent a half-dozen summers hanging out and playing open mics in the West Village—much later, a generation later than Rod, who was a respected singer-songwriter in the generation of new acoustic performers and writers in New York's Greenwich Village, beginning in the 1970s and '80s. So, when Rod shared with me his archives, I read and enjoyed the range of topics, moods, and tones of his nonmusical writings; some material struck me as a powerful and energetic story of that particular place. We then worked to publish *The Open Mike* (2014), a fictional treatment of Rod's own early musical mystery tours and colleagues. We hope the reader has—or will soon have—checked out *The Open Mike*.

In *The American Guerillas*, Rod MacDonald has produced a novel that can stand beside both popular fiction and experimental literary magical realism. There is something here for everyone who has ever enjoyed stimulating and provocative art of any kind. This was the book Rod held nearest to his heart, as he explains in his preface, and it's a kind of writing quite different from both his earlier fiction and his songs. And if Dylan Reed—the protagonist of *The American Guerillas*—finishes his odyssey by performing (for a lone audient) the first song he composed, that is certainly due to the elderly tribal woman who demands a song from him.

We hope you will enjoy both the fast action and slow, reflective paces of life portrayed in *The American Guerillas*. It will be the perfect gift for anyone who relishes both the momentary and the momentous little moments of time that are our privilege on this planet Earth.

Robert S. Koppelman, PhD
Senior Professor of English
Broward College, Ft. Lauderdale, Florida
January 2021

Preface

The American Guerillas began in autumn 1979, as an attempt to overcome my sadness after the death of my nephew, Brian Modica, at the age of eleven. The very first words I ever wrote for a work of fiction were the dedication to this book. From the very beginning, I imagined it as a would-be Hollywood movie, but my nephew's passing had awakened in me a spiritual curiosity and led me to every book about Native American life and philosophy I could get my hands on. A friend, David Donner, hired Tom Intondi to type the first draft in 1981, just so he could read it. Of the very small number of copies, one made it to Karen Garthe, a NYC poet and literary agent's assistant; Karen wisely advised me that, before trying to publish it, I should visit the areas described in the manuscript.

Thus, in summer 1981, I traveled across the US to the Sioux and Hopi reservations, and with a letter of introduction from Ms. Garthe, I met Frank Waters, author of *The Book of the Hopi.* Mr. Waters directed me to Thomas Banyaca, a Hopi who frequently spoke to the United Nations and other organizations about Hopi beliefs, including the Prophecy, a series of teachings on the past and future destructions of this world, when materialism, greed, and environmental damage have become irreversible. Mr. Banyaca graciously made me welcome in his home and gave me valuable insight into the simple yet majestic way of life the Hopi have practiced for hundreds of years. And that knowledge made it clear that my initial book was not a finished work.

Returning home to New York, I made intermittent attempts to complete the story but remained unsatisfied and probably would have given up but for the memory of my nephew. I continued working on it, and by 2006 had a new hand-typed manuscript. And now, thanks to software that enabled me to read the manuscript into a word processing program and edit it, there is a finished book.

Through all this time, I have resisted the urge to rewrite the dialogue, change the way essential things were first written, or explain the unexplainable, while, of necessity, correcting the grammar and some details. There is much about *The American Guerillas* that seems juvenile and amateurish to me now. There is also the joyousness and sense of discovery that the writer of 1979 to 1981, saddened and yet awakened by experience, wrote into these pages. I have done my best to leave it all intact. Whatever its inadequacies, my desire in publishing this work is to honor the promise to Brian that made me begin my first work of fiction. I hope that you, the reader, will find something of value in it as well.

Rod MacDonald
January 2021

Flashbacks

Remember Everything

HE PARKED THE CAR AND WALKED THE SINGLE STREET, LOOKING IN windows for the ghost of a familiar face. He tried the drugstore, but the old soda fountain was gone, replaced by a wall of cosmetics. He went into the grocery; the cashier, a young man in his twenties, stood behind the register in a white butcher's smock, smiling blandly and waiting for him to buy something. He rarely smoked but for some reason picked out a cigar and a small wooden box of matches, paid in silence, and put them in his shirt pocket.

He drove out of the village, remembering the way as clearly as ever, as if he were still riding his bicycle and gliding down the smooth black-top through the green trees, thick and fragrant with summer. And then, suddenly, there it was, encircled by the driveway and a few scattered fruit trees: the old white box house with its four-cornered roof. It was what he most remembered of Connecticut, and whenever someone spoke the word, he saw this old house with its rotting cherry tree on one side and lilac bushes on the other, sitting quietly on the unstripped road to the mountain.

There were no cars in the yard. He didn't know if anyone was home, but he went to the door and knocked. There was no answer, so he went into the yard and sat down on a green picnic table, planted in the grass. He took out the cigar and set it on the table; the matches, however, slipped through his fingers as he drew them from his pocket and landed on the grass at his feet. He bent down to pick them up, and a thin white roll of paper floated down.

He stared at it a moment before remembering the hitchhiker who'd reached across and dropped it into his shirt pocket last evening as he got out of the car in Pennsylvania.

"May you find everything you search for," the man had said, and now he whispered it quietly to himself. He was looking for old familiar things: Old Billy's house was still there, across the road to the left, where Old Billy would sit in a rocking chair all afternoon, reading the newspaper, while the neighborhood boys rode their bikes. They'd ride up his dirt driveway, walk to his chair, lean to his good ear, and ask for water. He'd take them out back to his white wooden well, its proud little roof freshly painted, and draw up a bucket of the best water anyone had ever tasted. He poured each glass with a smile for the boy who came to drink it. It was almost a daily ritual, conducted in virtual silence, but it made them better friends.

Across the street was a meadow that ran to the thick woods beyond. There was an abandoned bulldozer in the field, given a day off in the midst of digging a new road. Beyond it, the trees were unchanged. It might be their last days, and they still seemed like the edge of the world, so far from his house, if only because his father had told him that "never, not under any circumstances" should he go there, into those trees, that forest. And he never had.

But that was a long time ago.

He picked up the cigar and the joint, one in each hand, as if weighing them; he placed them both in his pocket and stood up.

And so Rett Haskins went for a walk. He crossed the street and followed the bulldozer's dirt track, stepping around mudholes from the last rain. Soon, he reached the trees, where he took a long look to each side; there seemed no break to them. But as he looked over the pine branches straight ahead, there was a narrow footpath. And so, pushing aside a low branch, and taking a deep breath, he stepped into the trees.

The woods were untouched by the development scarring the land by the road, and the sun, streaking through the white birches and pines, lent the scene a quiet serenity. He stood motionless, lost in thought and reverence, as his senses slowly awakened. Looking back, he realized he could not be seen from the road; he reached into his pocket, found the small cylinder of paper and the matches, took them out, and lit it, taking a long, slow drag.

As he watched the exhaled smoke drift like a miniature cloud through a sunbeam, a large cluster of mountain laurel appeared. He took a deep breath, inhaling the sweet fragrance of the pink blossoms. Walking slowly down the footpath, he pushed past a thistle of pine boughs and found himself in a clearing filled with lady's slippers, their single pink bulbs dangling on their single stems, forever teasing the long green leaves that reach out below them. And just as he caught his breath, exhaling, "Yes, yes," he spied that rare beauty: a white lady's slipper, surrounded by a field of pink, yet forever solitary. Its small white bulb glowed like a woman's breast in the moonlight. And soon he did not know how long he had stood there, as still as a deer, his thoughts entirely stopped, before the distinct, steady beat of water rushing over rocks made itself known to him.

He put the joint and matches back in his pocket and began walking, following the trail, until he found it: a stream twenty feet wide and running fast to his left, rippling over some small rocks. It seemed to gather force around each bend, until, to his surprise, it met another stream, where a rusty gate and an abandoned relic of an ancient small brick factory lay sinking into the tall grass. The combined streams swerved right, and he followed alongside, deeper into the green of summer, through the birch trees, the occasional oaks, and the glacial rocks scattered through the forest. The stream veered right as the trail continued straight on and, a few hundred yards later, rounded a large boulder. He looked ahead and froze. Beyond the overhanging roof of the thick, tall branches and leaves, there was a shining blue lake sparkling in the distance. He stopped, the sudden brightness dazzling him, and stood motionless, silent.

Starting as a speck, emerging from the mirror of the afternoon sun, something was moving on the water. As it drew closer toward the shore, Rett stepped behind a tree.

It was a canoe with two men in it, bare-chested, their black hair shaved along the sides and straight up on top. One man knelt in front, upright and watchful, while the other paddled noiselessly across the blue lake. Silhouetted by the reflected sunlight behind them, they created such a placid scene that he simply stared, as if they were a moving painting; they came ashore barefoot, sliding the canoe under a low canopy of leaves. They walked toward him before he could run without being seen, as he comprehended who they were.

The men in the canoe were Indians.

Lakker

———⟨∅/∅/∅⟩———

A S THE MEN MOVED FROM ONE CAMP TO ANOTHER, IT QUICKLY BECAME obvious the evacuation was not proceeding in an orderly fashion. The officers, standing beside the muddy, rut-filled road, their gear piled behind them, watched as the trucks, full of enlisted men, rolled by without stopping. When one of the transports went by empty, its driver staring straight ahead, Rett Haskins grabbed his pack and caught the passenger door from behind. He yanked the door open and threw his bag on the floor.

"Get the fuck out of here, Lieutenant," commanded the driver, stepping on the gas. Haskins swung back on the window frame, and when he reappeared in the doorway, he had a pistol.

"You are going to stop and pick up these officers here," he said, pointing the automatic at the large head and slick, woolly hair of Tank Lakker, his own soldier. He held it there while Lakker stopped, picking up the remaining stragglers, who might otherwise wander down the road until they got shot.

In a truck that had left earlier, some of the men thought they had succeeded in forgetting the officers.

"Sheeyit," one said, slapping fives in the back. "Did you see that mothafucka's face when we rolled on by? Did you see it? That mothafucka ain't never seen nothing like it."

"His mama and daddy ain't here to buy his way home," another followed.

5

"An' I sure ain't never seen no Viet Cong at no Ivy League pisshole," chimed in a third man, and they laughed. And it was true. Nothing in private schools or colleges had prepared these officers for anything they were expected to do in Vietnam, where there was little or no formation marching, salutes, football games, or tactical warfare. Yet here they were: white, privileged, educated, middle-class boys, twenty-two and twenty-three, stuck in the jungle to command squads of soldiers that were mostly black, poor, and streetwise. And though there were no streets here, they knew how to survive in the jungle far better than did the lieutenants—by making sure you were your own soldier, all the time, calling your own shots and watching out for your own ass. Let these dumb lieutenants send you out on patrol, and chances were good you wouldn't even see the shot that buried you.

Hardly anyone in this outfit saw the war anymore. There were a few patrols and occasional reports that the enemy was in the area, but there were never any battles. The Viet Cong fought the most classic style man had invented for defending his own turf: guerrilla warfare, one man at a time, never seen and never heard, felt only in the slow but steady death toll of GIs "lost in action," a phrase that meant nothing in this area of Vietnam. No, the real war to Haskins seemed to be right on his own base, between the haves and have-nots, the privileged and the ones who were stuck there because they had no power to do anything about it. Many of the enlisted men saw two enemies: the Viet Cong and the officers. The officers could get you in two ways, one because they were always the real enemy, with their fancy degrees, backgrounds, and ways of ordering you around—and because they could order you to do something that might get you blown away. Haskins acted by not acting; he never sent his men on patrol unless he was specifically ordered to, and then he kept them together in the safest place he could find. But they thought he was another stupid officer, with his university degree and his shaggy blond hair.

Of his men, Lakker was the quietest. To Haskins, he was also the most deadly; he'd be a great soldier if only he knew which war he wanted to fight. One night a friend of Haskins had gone to the officers' latrine. Someone had strung a wire across the pathway, and when the officer tripped, a flare went off that lit up the entire area; there was a short flurry of bullets, and the officer went down. No one knew who shot him or who rigged the wire; the Viet Cong were always thought to be around the base, and a flare was a clean setup for a bullet. But Haskins also knew that Lakker had told friends the dead officer was "better off where he was then sending us out on another fuckin' patrol."

The trucks rolled into camp. Haskins was tempted to say nothing to anyone about the incident and keep the officers in the truck, to watch and see how the enlisted men set up camp. He wanted to know how organized the idea had been to leave them in the jungle. But he jumped down and went into the captain's tent immediately and stayed a half hour. He was about two hundred yards down the path before someone dove at him from behind a tent, throwing him to the ground, hissing, "You motherfucker, I'm going to kill you for that."

Lakker had his hands on his throat, and Haskins was about to pass out, when he heard another voice say, coldly, "Give me one reason not to blow your head off right here, soldier."

Jim Quisto was pointing an automatic at Lakker's head, pressing it against his temple, and he continued to hold it there as Lakker rolled off Haskins onto the ground and curled into a ball. Moaning like a trapped and wounded animal, he crawled out from under the gun barrel, never looking Quisto in the eye. The gun still aimed at his head, he tripped and fell down. Visibly shaken, he got up again and held up his hands, backing away, turning as he made it around the tent, looking back over his shoulder one last time.

Quisto turned to Haskins, still holding the gun.

"You all right?"

"I'm okay. I don't know."

Haskins made it back to his tent. What a place, he thought. You can't tell whether you're supposed to shoot somebody you've never seen or the soldier next to you before he does it to you. He felt at a disadvantage because Lakker had nothing to lose, nothing to go back to but some streets he came from and because he hated him in a way he could never hate back, being painfully aware of his own privileged status.

He fell asleep, dreaming of the one person in this country who could soothe him, who was home in Da Lat right now, blowing out the candle by her own bed, wondering if he was all right.

Quisto woke him up early. It was still damp, and the mist hung just outside the camp. Haskins pulled on his pants and sat on the edge of the bed, as his friend stared at him, saying nothing.

"Something wrong, Jim?"

Silence.

"What's going on?"

"They found Lakker."

"What do you mean?"

"He was shot last night. On guard duty. He got a bullet in the side of the head. Sitting under a tree."

Neither of them said a thing. A bullet in the side of the head. It could have come from anywhere or from anyone. Lakker's number had come up: He'd survived his showdown with Quisto's automatic. Weakened, his bravado burst, he hadn't lasted through the night. Haskins put on his shirt.

"Did you do it?"

"No. Did you?"

"No."

They walked out into the camp. A pair of trucks were pulling out. A man in green ran by, calling out.

"The enemy is behind a ridge, three miles to the northwest!"

"Prove it," Rett said to no one, but Quisto turned, waiting.

"Prove to me that's where the enemy is," he said.

A Rodeo for Jimmy

—◦◦◦—

B Y THE YEAR 1977, EAST HAVERSACK, NEW JERSEY, HAD BECOME FAR less than the visionaries who moved there from New York City, anticipating the suburban utopia, had dreamed. In fact, it had become a nightmare, for slowly, throughout the '70s, a growing number of young children, ages eight to fifteen, had died of the disease leukemia. And there was one small group of businessmen who, faced with this fact, spent a great deal of money finding multiple things wrong with the children's organisms: pneumonia, anemia, anything that would complicate the medical reports and make the cause of their sickness seem less evident. These resourceful citizens were the owners of East Haversack's only industry: a metachloride plant squatting on a hill to the southwest of town.

Since the wind, coming off the Jersey Hills, bore the invisible smell of the plant most of the time, most of the residents and nearly all of the parents of the deceased children were convinced the plant was responsible for their children dying. But leukemia is a hard disease to trace, and every effort to close the plant was thwarted by judges who, unwilling to read between the lines, ruled there was "no conclusive evidence that the plant was exclusively responsible" for the epidemic. And no doctor could show that those millions of white blood cells that wouldn't go away were directly linked to the plant. Still, a parent who sees his child degenerate before his eyes needs a lot less evidence than a federal judge.

Jim Quisto was one of those parents, having lost a twelve-year-old son in 1980. He wrote to Rett Haskins, "There is no law here in East Haversack, where a small group of people will continue to make these chemicals and make these children die, because no one has the money to finance the expertise to prove what is going on."

Heading east on the train, Haskins was restless, thinking of what he owed his Vietnam sidekick. He took a cab from the station, and a short ride later, the two old friends were reunited. He shook hands with Quisto's wife, Joan, a friendly dark-haired woman in her early thirties, who quickly left them alone after a dinner of stories, memories, and good cheer. The two men took a short walk to the car and a short drive to a nearby bar and had a round of beers before Haskins said, "Let's keep going."

"Any place in particular?"

"Yes. I want you to see the metachloride plant."

Two or three miles passed in silence. Finally, Haskins asked, "Want to tell me about it?"

"Not much to tell," Quisto answered. "Jimmy started having problems one day with routine things—getting up, going to school. He said he felt sick a lot. We took him to a doctor and ran some tests. Next thing is, they took him to a hospital. Said it was leukemia. During the next few months, they give them all sorts of treatments, chemotherapy, radiation, even sent him home twice, saying he had a remission. He died about three months after the last time he had to go back.

"My wife and I go to visit his grave every Sunday before we go to church. She says she understands. But I don't."

They got to the factory site a minute later. It was not much to look at, an old brick hulk on an otherwise uninhabited stretch of grass; what interested him most was how it was secured. There was a six-foot fence for a perimeter, one single driveway curling around back, a guard at the gate, and three ribbons of barbed wire along the top of the fence. The yard was lit with spotlights from every corner of the building, but the plant was dark.

"Tell me, Jim, how many other kids are there in this town like Jimmy?"

"Last count I know of was seventeen. Why?"

"Do you think their parents feel like you do?"

"Some of them."

"Do you ever get together and talk about doing something about it?"

"Like what? We get together, but we've never really had that kind of sentiment together. Do you have something in mind? Is that why you came here?"

The next day, Quisto and Haskins sat down and ran through the names of fathers of kids who had died of leukemia in East Haversack. He knew most of them but only four well; of these, he felt only three could be trusted to keep a secret, a secret they could not even tell their wives. They were Jack Tasker, who worked with Quisto in Newark; Frank Atwater, a black man who had also served in Vietnam; and Tass Wilcox, a construction worker in the area's office building trades. They ruled out the fourth because, although they had no reason not to trust him, none of the men had ever worked, fought, or drank alongside him enough to feel safe. They were being careful.

The next night, they met in Quisto's basement. The occasion was a card game with the boys to celebrate Haskins' visit.

"Whose deal?"

They handed him the cards. Dealer's choice.

"I want to play rodeo."

"Another new game? What's that?"

"It's a tactic used for taking out an enemy installation."

"This is a card game?"

He put down the deck.

"Jim says you can all be trusted. So here it is: Are you willing to hear something that can't leave this room?

The three men looked at their neighbors.

"What's this about?"

Jim Quisto looked at his friends and at Rett.

"I think what he means is, if you stay, you can never talk about this with anyone. Period."

There was a prolonged silence. Finally, Tasker leaned forward and said, "I think I know where this is going. And I'll stay."

Each of the others pulled his chair forward. They were all in. Whatever it was.

"We want to take out the plant south of town. You all know why. We want to blow it up." He sounded much more confident than he felt, waiting for someone to break the dead silence.

Tasker spoke first.

"Do you think this is the right thing to do? We all know about this plant, and your son, Jim. And mine. But is this right?"

"It's either that or it'll be there forever. There is no legal way to close it. It's been tried. You can't prove anything. There's nothing but that smell and the sinking feeling I get when it's in the air."

They were all quiet.

"This isn't the first time I thought of it myself," Wilcox volunteered. "It's a sore right there. And we do know how to do it—between us. We can't just do this out of revenge, though. It's got to be the best thing to do. If it is, I'm with you all the way."

Quisto cleared his throat.

"Look, nothing will bring back Jimmy or any of the other kids. But what about all the others that have a right to grow up? You can't move. Anyplace is likely to have the same problem. I think we can do something about it right here. A citizens' action. Nice and clean, no dead bodies, no getting caught. We have to plan it. Rett came here with this idea. I'm … I'm surprised to think of actually doing it. But I've come to think we should. Do it."

Only Atwater had remained silent.

"Frank?"

"These are chemicals, guys. I did some demolition work, and one of the big problems is getting out before it all blows. Plus, what will happen when all those toxic things hit the air? Will it wipe out a lot of innocent people?"

"I checked this out a few months ago," Wilcox put in. Eyebrows went up around the table. He shrugged. "Got to drinking one night with one of the fellows there. He said the plant has a secret evacuation plan filed with the police. Well, why shouldn't it? It's an old building and might even blow on its own."

"You know they'll rebuild it," Tasker said. "This will be symbolic more than anything."

They thought that over.

"Maybe the environmental people can fight that or at least make them clean it up. Okay then. I told Rett it's all or nothing. We don't do it unless we're all in. Anybody want to leave right now? No questions asked, no pressure."

They all stayed.

For a few seconds, they looked at each other with new eyes.

"You said something about a rodeo. How does that work?" Wilcox asked.

"It's a team effort. First man in is the cattle roper; he ties up the outside guard. The second man rides the steer; that is, he draws the interior people out into the open. The third guys are the bronco busters; they take out the interior guards once they are exposed. Then you take the bull by the nuts and blow the place.

"We don't want anyone hurt. We'll have to subdue the guards and take them somewhere else. Understood?" They all nodded.

Tasker looked at Wilcox.

"You sure there's an evacuation plan for this community?"

"Well, I don't think I should ask around just before we do it. But I'm pretty sure."

"Okay, so we'll call the police right before the first explosion. That'll give them some time."

There were footsteps on the stairs. Joan Quisto walked in with a tray of fresh beers. Rett scooped up the cards.

"Five-card stud. Winner take all," he grinned.

༄

Since Haskins was the only one who had never been seen before in East Haversack, he would inspect the plant. He called ahead to inquire about a job, answering enough questions to sound as if he knew what he was doing, and got an appointment. The interview lasted half an hour and got him a "maybe," and as he left the personnel office, he noticed something strange: he had a long corridor to walk down by himself. Seizing the opportunity, he slipped down a stairway until he got to the basement. It was empty. One of his Vietnam skills had been electronics; that is, he had some ideas of circuitry and knew a few types of power boxes. If there was an alarm system in this plant, it would be here, and at some point, it would have to be neutralized. Haskins didn't care so much if it was designed to stop a robbery or to sound an alarm; his main concern was whether it contained a direct hookup to the police.

The main boxes were old and looked as if they hadn't been modernized since the plant was built. He pried them open carefully, leaving no marks. He was not about to make anybody think they'd been opened. One contained a large horseshoe-shaped handle. He guessed that was either a main circuit breaker, or if necessary, it sounded an alarm. The other he hadn't seen before; it was functioning constantly, though, by the low hum it put out, and inside was a simple powerpack that had no open wires or fuses. He traced the wires from the sides of the box; they were routed out through cables and ran almost all the way around the basement walls, meeting in another large box. This one was simpler: labeled "siren," it contained an on-off switch and was probably connected to an alarm or a siren that would sound if the fence were cut. Or if the grounds were entered at night or a door was opened. But he saw nothing that looked like an outside connection.

He went upstairs again. Reentering the hallway, he met the personnel director.

"Still here?"

"I've been a little sick. I had to spend some time in the bathroom."

"The bathroom is the other way, down there."

"I didn't know that. I found one on the floor below."

He didn't hang around to be more convincing. Driving out, he looked along the fence. It had small insulator terminals at the four corners. At the gate, he shut off his engine, got out, and lifted the hood as the gatekeeper came over.

"Damn car, stalls all the time," he said. Disgusted with the machine, he unscrewed the wingnut from the air filter and flung it at the fence, where it sparked as it hit. Electric fence. He jammed his finger in the carburetor and rattled it around. The gatekeeper just stared. On the third floor of the plant, the personnel director watched the scene, amused. Something was making that young man very nervous, he thought. He would not be a good risk to be around dangerous materials, and he would not get the job.

"It's an electric fence wired to an alarm. Not much security—a guard or two. Doesn't seem to be an attitude that the plant has anything to be secured against. My guess is, nobody on duty at night except a handful of janitors and a gatekeeper."

Meanwhile, the others had taken care of their preparations. Tasker's job was to boost a car, a skill he had learned in his high-school years well enough to draw some probation.

"A cinch. You never forget how, like riding a bicycle," he grinned.

Atwater had handled explosives in Vietnam, and he showed them a demo model, as he called it: a small but lethal charge that, when placed in the main power generators, would generate enough heat to blast open the first floor and start a major fire with a high enough temperature to outlast anything the East Haversack fire department might have handy.

"Now, this little mother," he said, smiling, "is going to be hooked to this little fuse here. We will have seven minutes to get the hell out of there."

"Will that take out the whole plant?"

"Hard to say. I've kept in touch with this group in Pennsylvania that likes to think they're still commandos. This weekend I'm seeing one of them, so I'll get a couple of grenades, too. But those go off right away; we'll be there at the time if we have to use them."

Wilcox would be, with Haskins, the main bronco buster. His job was to get the janitors out of the factory. But to where?

"Can you boost a van, Jack?"

"No sweat."

"Any place to leave the whole bunch—truck, guard, janitor?"

"There is an unmanned dump over in Patterson."

On the following Tuesday, a full moon shone as four men waited; a van pulled up, no rear windows, one driver. They walked over and got in.

"Anyone see you?"

"Nope. Parking garage, automatic checkout system."

In fifteen minutes, they were approaching the edge of East Haversack, just outside of town atop a small hill. Four men crouched in the back as the driver pulled up to the gatehouse. Tasker rolled down his window and called to the guard, who stared as if he had never seen anyone during his shift before.

"I'm lost. Can you tell me how to get to the Lincoln Tunnel?"

The guard came toward the window. Meanwhile, the rear door of the van opened quietly, and Quisto, the cattle roper, crept out. He needed to reach the guard before he had a good look at Tasker's face, and the unsuspecting guard saw nothing as Quisto put the handkerchief saturated with chloroform firmly over his mouth and nose. He was out instantly. Quickly, they lifted him into the van and began tying him up. They put on ski masks and gloves and drove slowly up to the factory.

Wilcox, Haskins, and Atwater got out and moved out of view of the front door. They would need to know how many men were inside, pushing brooms or minding meters. Tasker honked the horn. An old janitor came out, half bent over and walking slowly. Wilcox and Atwater grabbed him from behind, led him around behind the van, and handed him a 3 × 5 card.

In capital letters, it said, "CAN YOU READ THIS?"

The man, shaking, nodded.

"HOW MANY INSIDE?" read the second card.

"Five," the man answered, holding up five fingers. The factory door opened, and a janitor was there. For a second everyone froze. Some intuition told him something was wrong, and he turned and went inside, unsure if he should run for the alarms or act as if he hadn't seen anything. Wilcox and Haskins went after him, catching him halfway down the hall. Wilcox had the chloroform on him before he had time to whimper. Four to go.

Atwater, following a sketch Haskins had drawn from his previous visit, made for the stairs. Wilcox and Haskins followed the long corridor. At the end, in a small office, a light was on.

"Come on in," a male voice began, but at the sight of two men in masks, the middle-aged black man ducked behind a desk and let out a yell. Quickly, they were on him with the chloroform, and he was out. They waited. Footsteps coming closer signaled two more arriving; the door opened and two uniformed guards entered, no weapons drawn, as if unaware of the fight that had preceded them. Wilcox and Haskins each jumped one; the two surprised men were no match for the intruders and were quickly overpowered. Haskins chloroformed his. Wilcox decided to gamble.

"Where's the other janitor?"

"In the basement." Wilcox put him out. They headed for the stairs, hearing nothing. They pushed open the door and saw a light down a narrow corridor. They walked softly toward it and pushed open the door. Inside, Atwater was rigging a wire fuse up over a pipe. At his feet was the crumpled body of the remaining janitor, seemingly unconscious but breathing.

"Sorry, no time to mess around," Atwater shrugged as he worked on the wires. "Why don't you throw this guy in the truck and wait for me?"

Haskins lifted the man onto his shoulder. Back upstairs, Wilcox got to the room with the two other bodies as one was crawling toward a telephone. He kicked the man's arm, sent him sprawling, then dosed them both again with the chloroform.

In the basement, Atwater connected the last of his fuses to the main power terminal. He hoped this would circulate through the entire electrical system and, in case the other explosives he had set didn't do the job, start a bonfire. The other charges were in vulnerable spots, one near a fuel storage area, one near some exhaust ventilators, and the first one, the most delicately set up of the bunch, near the central heating system. The U.S. Army had taught him well, and he went around the large basement room and made the last connections on each charge. They would have seven minutes to get the hell out of there.

By the time they hit the main floor, Wilcox and Haskins were searching frantically for the first guard, who had disappeared.

"What? Where?" They split up. Six minutes. Haskins started on the bathrooms. Wilcox went upstairs. Atwater found him trying to make it to a telephone right in one of the front offices; he'd been hiding the whole time in the next room. He approached the man across a desk, only his eyes visible behind the mask, the man terrified. Finally, he lunged to the right; the man went for the door, and he pulled back from his feint. Standoff. They were running out of time. He jumped onto the large desk, faked right, and jumped on the man as he ran around to his left. He hit his head against the desk to put him out.

Haskins heard the commotion and arrived; they dragged the guard into the hallway and outside to the van.

"Three minutes. Three minutes. Three minutes," Atwater was shouting. Wilcox appeared in a second-floor window.

"Got him?"

"Get out of there."

"Be right down."

"There's no time. Jump!" Wilcox hesitated a second. "Jump, you asshole, jump!" Wilcox pulled his legs out through the window, looked down once, yelled "Shiiiit," and jumped. He hit the asphalt and doubled over. Atwater grabbed him and threw them in the van.

Inside, two of the captives were waking up. Quisto poured some more green liquid on a handkerchief and stuffed it in their faces, and as the van pulled out of the empty yard onto the roadway, the first explosion hit like a distant gunshot, muffled, nothing showing.

"Better do more than that," Atwater mumbled to himself. Then there were two more, quickly, faintly, with still no visible sign. He was worried. All this and he wanted the place leveled.

Tasker turned the van around and stopped. A third series of soft explosions went off as they stared through the windshield.

"Look." From a window, the first flames broke out. Then the last explosion went off. This one they saw. The front windows blew out, then two on the side. A sidewall of the basement, just above the ground, fluffed out like a sack of sawdust. That side of the building sagged. A beam fell down, flames shot out through the opening, and then it was too risky to hang around. Out of sight of the plant, they heard a final— and the loudest—crashing sound as even the van shuddered. The sky behind them was bright orange, as pinpoints of reflected flames danced across the windows of houses in the narrow valley.

They had done it.

Sirens faded in the distance as Tasker took a long way around, using back roads, avoiding downtowns or settled areas. They stopped in some woods a few miles from the plant and pushed out seven sleeping bodies. Ten minutes later, they pulled into an abandoned dump beneath the Patterson full moon and got out of the van. Tasker wiped everything down, then collected the ropes, gloves, masks, chloroform and rags, and tossed them into an empty barrel. He squirted some fluid over the pile and tossed in a match; they watched the fire erupt, climbed into a station wagon and drove away.

Search and Destroy

—◈◈◈—

HASKINS GOT BACK TO CHICAGO ON THE AFTERNOON TRAIN. HE took the Clark Street bus to the near North Side, stopping at his apartment just long enough to drop his pack, and headed a few blocks west to the Seminary Restaurant. He picked at some fish, potatoes, and salad, wondering over and over again if what they had done was right or wrong. But it was done. He dragged dinner out for two hours, expecting to see a familiar face any time, but none came, and when he finally gave up, it was seven o'clock and almost dark outside.

Before he left the restaurant, he called Lina, who would be waiting to hear from him, and when he got to his apartment building, she was standing outside. Lena was a WASP with soul, a classic American beauty with long blond hair, wide-open green eyes, and a great slender figure, and she couldn't stand around the street for very long without some man making his move. As Haskins came around the corner, he saw a familiar sight: a mid-twenties, dark, sunglassed driver in a sportscar a few lengths away, getting together his rap to pull up to the long-legged beauty standing on the sidewalk. Haskins and the car arrived together; Rett took her inside immediately, noticing, as he always did, that she gave the man in the car no attention. It wasn't easy to love a beautiful woman; he knew he couldn't keep on with her if her head were constantly turned by the men her beauty drew out.

They talked meaninglessly for a few minutes; he told her he had been to see an old buddy from the army, and when she walked over and kissed him, he knew he was off the hook. They went inside to the bedroom, and he almost forgot his trip east in the pleasure of undressing this beautiful woman who loved him, slowly going over her entire body with his hands, kissing her breasts and stomach, and gently probing her with his tongue. She tried twice to take him inside her, but he made her wait and held her, kissed her, until he entered her and they made love, slowly and softly. Both managed to climax, and when she kissed him all over his face, he knew it was going to be all right. Within a few minutes, she was asleep, but Haskins continued staring blankly into the ceiling for a long time.

After a while, he got too restless to lie still. He looked over at Lena. A faint light coming in the window made her face shine, as if it were being painted by a portrait artist whose fame would live in it for centuries. He didn't want to wake her; silently, he slipped from under the sheet and crept barefoot to the bedroom door and knew she was still sleeping when he closed it and turned on the kitchen light. Small, dark movements caught his eye across the room and beneath the table on which he ate. He had gone away, leaving his coffee maker filled with coffee, and it had leaked a large, sticky brown stain that had expanded to half the tablecloth. He pulled the table out; the stain had soaked the cloth, and, wedged against the wall, had stayed wet and grown mildew. Roaches scattered frantically along the wall and baseboard. He pushed the table back into place so they wouldn't have to escape.

It was 10:45. Haskins put on some shoes and his jacket and went outside. The corner grocery might still be open, so he headed there; it was closed. He flagged down a passing cab.

"Where's there a grocery open right now?" he asked.

"Over on Halsted," the man replied in a thick accent, "about three dolla." He got in. The grocery had only one brand of spray bomb for bugs, one of the toxic commercial varieties, but the job had to be done even if it meant stinking the place out. He bought a can and started walking back. The only other person in the store—in an army jacket, long, stringy hair, and sandals—caught up outside.

"You know, that stuff will get into your food chain, man," he began. "You'll be eating it in a few days."

"I'm not planning on eating roaches," Haskins said.

"But some of them won't die. They develop an immunity to the spray, and then when they walk around, they leave it on your dishes and silverware."

Haskins made a note to himself to wash everything he used for the next couple of weeks.

"You ought to try something else," the man went on.

"Such as?"

"Boric acid, roach motels, anything else." He began a long rap on the food chain, but as they passed a local taco shop, Haskins excused himself and ducked inside. He played a game of pinball, some space-age game with torpedoes shooting down aliens from other planets; whenever you sent the ball around the loop in the top, you got a double bonus. He was just approaching the score for a free game when he sent the ball up to the top again, and it stuck on a metal trigger. He tried shaking the machine back and forward, but the ball was lodged and wouldn't move. Finally, he jiggled it to the side. Tilt. He brought his fist down and said, "Damn!" and the glass cracked loudly. He watched the ball shake loose of the trigger and dribble lamely down the center hole. End of game.

The restaurant was empty; a radio played in the kitchen. He turned and left.

At home, he walked into the kitchen, flicked on the light, and saw small dark movements across the room again. He took off his jacket, closed the bedroom door tightly, and broke the seal on the spray can. He sprayed a large circle around the table on the wall, twice, until whatever was behind it was completely encircled with spray. He then sprayed a line diagonally across the floor; if any were to get away, they would have to cross the spray first. He got a broom handy and prepared for a frontal assault.

In one fast movement, he pulled the table out from the wall, yanked off the tablecloth, and shook it above the circle he'd sprayed. Roaches rained down and began running crazily around, first one perimeter of the circle, then to the next, unable to get away; dozens more were on the wall. Haskins felt the puke rising in his throat but fought it down; he pounded on the table with his fist three times as more books fell onto the floor, their stench rising toward him. He had them pinned in a circle and was about to let them have it when the phone started ringing. He ignored it. He brought his foot down and squashed clusters of bugs at a time, trying to use as little spray as possible. Two roaches broke through the circle and headed across the floor; he nailed them with his foot.

The spray had dried a bit; he would need to spray more. This time, he reached down and pointed the nozzle right at them, making a quick circle, blasting them point-blank. Within seconds, he had hit every bug he could see, and the smell was making him gag. He reached into a drawer and found a handkerchief, made a bandit's mask of it, and tied it around his face so it covered his nose and mouth. As he finished, the last cockroaches were dying, twitching miserably on the floor with the lethal spray on their bodies until they flipped over like cartoon carica-tures, feet up, on their backs. Haskins realized he was alone in the room; everything else was dead. He was breathing hard. He walked away for a few seconds, then grabbed the broom and began sweeping up.

And then he saw them.

Up on the wall, across the top of the frame of his imitation Picasso of Don Quixote, they sat like birds on the wire, their antennas twitch-ing: another thirty cockroaches at least, enough to breed into hundreds in days. Black birds without sunlight, crows without corn, they were making their nests in his kitchen, planting their gardens in his garbage, assuming their highways in his water pipes; and they were watching him trample, spray bomb, and sweep up their dead comrades, knowing they could produce more of those insect bodies in a few days than he could possibly kill. For this was war; it was his apartment or theirs, and both sides knew it.

Haskins yanked a folding chair from the other room to the wall where the painting hung. He opened the door to the apartment and left it open. Not one roach can escape, he thought. He jumped on the chair, took the picture down and ran for the door. Two bugs jumped off, onto the floor; he stamped them with his feet. He made the hallway with the others still on the frame, but in the brightly lit hallway they began jumping off, and he had to stomp another ten to keep them from reentering the apartment. He made the street with the rest intact and bashed the edge of the frame on the sidewalk, until the other bugs bounced off, until he saw there were none left.

He went back inside, began sponging their stink off the edging and frame, and hung it back up. But his shoes still had the smell of death on them.

Taking no chances, he grabbed the spray can again, opened the doors beneath the sink, and saw another colony of bugs scatter. He opened fire. These were bugs that came and went in the dark, and could not squeeze out of the storage area fast enough to get out; he killed them all, twitching and spinning like turkeys with their heads cut off. What a way to die, he thought; give me a quick bullet with no smell, please. He crossed the kitchen and tore open the oven door, but for once, there was no enemy to kill. He went back to the sink and shot blindly into the space up behind the drainage basin, filling the air with insecticide; instantly, more roaches dropped out to the bottom, landing feet up, legs out, gasping soundlessly. Take no prisoners, he thought, and shot into every spot around the sink that he could not see; at each juncture, they tumbled out and died. He had to get every one; there could be no surrender, no civilians, no white flags, no chance to breed more of this sickening enemy.

Finally, they were all dead. They had to be dead. There was no place left to hide. Haskins was reeling from the smell. But he picked up the broom and began sweeping up the dead by the dozens onto a piece of cardboard used as a dustpan, shoveling loads of roaches into a brown paper bag. He worked quickly and was soon finished, and he carried the bag out to the street, came back, and took an old shirt and soaked it with water. Then he wiped the wall, the table, the floor, the sink, and the water pipes, a process that took several minutes. It was easily 2:00 a.m. when he was done according to the clock on the wall above the refrigerator, when a solitary cockroach appeared on the wall, heading for a crack where the wall and ceiling joined that must have been ten feet away. The roach was staggering, walking in an uneven line, a survivor somehow escaping Haskins' fury; and it was white, pure white, so that its edges seemed almost luminous, for this bug had grown up in darkness as an albino, not venturing out to forage through human garbage for a meal but a creature of the cracks and pipes that connected the human colony of this building. Haskins reached up instinctively and squashed it with his thumb, then stared at his thumb for a moment before washing it off in the sink. And finally, he went into the bathroom, knelt down in front of the toilet, and threw up.

When he had finished heaving, he hung his head, and, soundlessly, tears came to his eyes. He was kneeling there, shaking and crying, a man who had witnessed human beings blown away in the dark, a man who had once drunkenly boasted he could laugh in death's face, crying like an idiot over the toilet bowl. And it was minutes, hopeless minutes, of shaking and being unable to stand up before he felt a hand on his shoulder, before he felt her kneeling down behind and putting her arms around him, before she rested her head against his back.

"Rett," she said. "Rett. It's all right. It's all right."

The Journey of the Indian

——⊙/⊙/⊙——

N O MAN CAN TRULY OWN LAND. HE CAN, GIVEN THE SHELTER OF
the government that recognizes his territorial boundary, occupy and
even leave it to his heirs, but once that shelter falls, his ownership is a
mere piece of paper. From Russia to China to Cuba or back to the lives
of those first white settlers in North America, ownership has proven no
deterrent to war, greed, circumstance, or revolution.

It is often said that the American Indians understood this fact, that
the earth belonged to itself and not to men and should be treated with
respect for the abundance it gave men in return. The European kings,
however, thought that by sticking a flag in the ground one claimed whole
continents as well as all the natural resources and subjects. First the Dutch
and the English, then the Spanish and English, until finally only the
French stood between the English and possession of all North America
east of the Mississippi. Given, then, promises of independence and land
from the French king, the Indians fought white Englishmen, a continuing
battle they would reenact for another century and a half, always losing,
always being pushed off the land they knew no man could own.

Rett Haskins stood behind a tree beside the river, expecting to be
seen any moment. He began to step into plain view when he was grabbed
from behind and yanked unceremoniously to the ground.

"Get down, you imbecile," whispered a very British voice. "Do you
want an arrow between the eyes?"

Haskins stayed on the ground, watching the two Indians vanish into the forest. Still on the ground, the other man said, "Right, then, who the bloody hell are you, and what are those clothes?"

Rett reacted by looking at his own shirt and blue jeans, a seemingly normal mode of dress. They stood up. The other man wore deerskin, a hat looking like a furball on his head, and a pouch hanging on a long strap from his right shoulder to his hips. And in his hands was a long, rustic-looking rifle.

"What the hell is going on? Is this some kind of reenactment? Or a masquerade party?" Haskins demanded. "And who are you?"

"My name is Christoph, Gov, but that's no concern of yours. You'd better come with me." Drawing a knife, a footlong sliver of steel, he beckoned Rett to move. Haskins walked in front as they moved quickly along the trail, toward the lake, then following the shore to a clearing where the river left the lake and flowed out into the trees. And there stood a small fortress, built of birch and pine log strapped together, barely as big around as a medium-sized apartment house.

"Things are quiet now, mate," said Christoph, pointing to the small squad of men sitting outside the fort. These men were wearing red uniforms and holding strange-looking tall hats; and as he approached, they watched wide-eyed, equaling Haskins' own astonishment.

"We'll see the major, mate," the deerskin-clad man said. "Just a minute." He went over to the men and whispered something, pointing off into the trees; they nodded and gave him a large jug, which he gratefully raised to his lips, swigged, and returned. Two of them walked over, and as Christoph guarded them, they searched Rett's pockets and patted him down. They found the cigar and matches, passing them to Christoph, who held them in his hands as they entered the fort. They walked through a small collection of rolled-up bundles and a few uniformed men at a firepit; near the center of the fort stood a man with gold braids around one arm.

"Major, I found this man wandering in the woods."

"Good work, Christoph. What did he tell you?" asked the major without looking up.

"Nothing, sir. He got righteous angry, he did."

"Tie him up and fasten him to the tree over there, then."

"And he had these on him."

The major looked up. He saw the extended hand, holding the cigar and matches, and took them up, turning them over as if examining them. With sudden inspiration, he held the cigar up to his nose and breathed in.

"Tobacco," he mused aloud, handing it back to Christoph. "Here, you have it. I don't like the stuff." But he put the matches in a side pocket of his jacket.

"Major, sir, with no disrespect meant to you, sir, I think you had better talk to him."

The major saw a well-dressed man in blue jeans and sports shirt. No gun, no hat, no pouch. He squinted.

"Casca say?" he asked.

"What?"

"Do you speak English?"

"Of course I do. What is this place? Who are you people?"

"This is, sir, Fort Quinnipiac, named after this river, right here on the shores of this lake. And you are its prisoner."

"For what?"

"You, sir, are a prisoner of war. Since you are out of uniform, you will be shot as a spy as soon as we are through questioning you. Now, what's your name?"

"Wait a minute. I'm no spy. Spy for whom? What's going on? I was walking in the woods, and suddenly there's a river that's out of nowhere, a huge lake, a fort, and all these soldiers, and you call me a spy!"

The major squinted.

"This is some reenactment, one of those battle groups, right?"

"What's your name?"

"And who are these Indians? There haven't been Indians in this part of Connecticut for two hundred years," he continued.

"Where did you say there are no Indians?"

"Connecticut. This state."

This time, the major blinked.

"I've heard the word 'Connecticut'. The Indians say it means 'shining water.' It's their name for big river a few miles away. But what do you mean by 'this state'?"

"I grew up here. This state is called Connecticut. So is the river. Where do these Indians come from?"

"They're the Quinnipiacs. And since they didn't kill you in the woods, they must know you. But your English is good. Curious, that accent. Now, what's your name? Answer me!" the major shouted, and the camp grew quiet. The major looked around and was not embarrassed.

"Come over here," he said, leading Rett to a vacant corner of the fort. "Now, let me give you a few seconds to try and save your life. We have a patrol out, and I can't spend all day at it."

"My name is Rett Haskins. I don't know who you are or what's going on. Is this real shooting you are doing or some elaborate wargame? I'm not a spy. If anything, I'm an accidental prisoner here who doesn't even know who's fighting."

"Mr. Haskins—if that is your name—there is indeed a war going on. My superiors, more recently arrived to it than myself, say that in England they call this the French and Indian War. The shooting is certainly real, and the Indians would certainly kill you if they thought you were English. Have you been asleep for fifty years or something? Are you playing some game with me? I assure you, you will lose."

But Haskins was already unable to contain himself.

"The French and Indian War? That was more than two hundred years ago!"

"I beg your pardon?"

They left him in the fort with a small armed guard. The rest of the men went on patrol, staying close to the structure, fanning out until, almost at nightfall, they returned, wondering among themselves where the enemy was, an enemy that could be unseen and unheard until the instant an arrow cut through a soldier's chest. There were about a hundred men there, and at night the fort was very crowded, but Haskins fell asleep despite the snoring. In the morning, he was brought to the major again.

"Now, Haskins. You say you know what this Connecticut River is. Can you lead us there?"

He had driven across it on the way to the beach.

"It's twenty miles or so, Major, a long ways on foot."

"Nonsense. How do you suppose we got here? We start tomorrow. But I assure you, should you attempt any tricks or signal to the Indians, or if I come to believe you are leading us in circles, I'll waste no time shooting you myself. Understood?"

But the next day, an arrow flew out of the trees and killed one of the stockade guards. A dozen men immediately ran toward the woods, firing their muskets into the trees. Haskins went over to the dead man. He was really dead, the point deeply embedded in his chest.

"A good man," a voice said.

"Aye," said another.

"Haskins," said the major. "Carry him over there by the stockade and bury him. Get a shovel from the corporal."

He was sent at gunpoint outside the gate, along a wall of pine logs standing on end, unguarded but observed from behind the wall. Perhaps it was a test: If he ran, they would shoot him down, and if he stayed, they might believe him, although he wasn't sure anymore what he believed. He prayed no arrows would cut him down while he dug; though every thin sound in the trees and underbrush terrified him, he saw and heard no Indians and finished the job frightened but unharmed. Then he went to the major, for he had been thinking.

"Major, what I have to say is rather far-fetched, but I think you should hear it before you kill me or do whatever you have planned."

"All right, then. Go ahead."

"First of all, I came walking in the woods across the street from my family's old house. I've been away many years."

"Where?"

"California, Chicago—it isn't important—but first, I need some honest answers. Do you know what a hand grenade is?"

"Some weird knife, perhaps?"

"No, Major. Have you ever heard of Vietnam?"

"No."

"Do you know what an automobile is?"

"An automobile? Let's see, mobile, something that moves, auto, something you move yourself?"

"Not exactly. Major, in the last twenty years, I have fought in Asia, driven an automobile—which is a metal carriage with an engine—and used a hand grenade that could blow this entire stockade up in three seconds. These things mean nothing to you?"

The major took off his hat and scratched his head.

"Major, when I entered these woods, it was a summer day in 1980. That's 1980, Major. Do you keep a calendar? What day is this for you?"

The man's eyes narrowed. He stood up and barked, "I don't know what you expect to gain by this. It's 1762, five August. Christoph! Over here at once!"

The scout hustled over. He was the only other man there not in a red uniform.

"What day is today, Christoph?" he asked.

"I don't rightly know the date, sir, but I think it's August. August 1762."

"Thank you, Christoph. Dismissed." He turned to Haskins. "Now, sir, you had better explain yourself."

"I can't, Major. When I left the street—never mind that—when I started walking in these woods, it was 1980. There was no war. This war is one I read about in history books when I was in grade school."

The major squinted.

"Who wins?"

"The English."

"Do you believe that?"

"I know it. It's a historical fact."

"Then I give you a choice. Take a uniform and wear it as one of us, and we'll say you wandered into our battle. Or we shoot you. If what you say is true, you don't belong here. But if we let you leave, either the Indians will kill you or, if you're one of the French, they'll take you to their *capitaine*. Neither of those is acceptable, so you have to stay. And be a soldier."

"But I have no quarrel with anyone."

"My dear sir. This is war. It does not matter if you personally have any quarrels at all. You are going to fight either with us or against us. The choice is yours, although since you are already our prisoner, if you choose to be against us, you will be shot."

"All right, I'm with you." The ease with which he said it surprised him, but he had seen modern warfare. Could he face arrows and muskets? At least long enough to escape?

The major, whose name was Gilley, had not given up the idea of reaching the Connecticut River, the land of shining water. He reasoned that the other British garrisons would be there also at some key juncture with supplies and munitions and replacements for his men, who otherwise would have been left in the woods by the British commanders. Four days later, they emerged from the woods around the lakeside, marching east along the lakefront, toward the deepening sun; if the Indians were paying attention, they remained hidden, and Haskins had seen no French at all. He hoped the land would resemble what he knew as a boy, when his father had taken him climbing on Saturdays. Now, when the troop reached the hilltop and could see for some distance, he recognized the high rock to the east. In the twentieth century, the residents of a small city on the other side called it West Peak and put a radio tower and a castle on top, but now it was a naked slab of rock above the tree line, whose sole purpose was to keep Haskins from being shot as a spy.

"Major Gilley," he said, "that point is the first bearing. The river will be ten to fifteen miles beyond it, flowing north and south. There will be a clear passage about half a mile to the south of the mountain peak and flat terrain after that. There's only one problem."

"And that is?"

"The passage is narrow. It's a perfect spot for an ambush."

Gilley sent Christoph ahead, and they set out, Haskins leading them along what would someday be the main roads in his hometown, working from memory and intuition. They made three miles with no problems and were drawing close to the mountain. He even began to feel comfortable in the red uniform, with the powder pouch and the tall hat. He had not fired his musket yet, although he'd been instructed in muzzle loading and aiming it, and he wondered if it worked. That seemed too trusting for Major Gilley, who still couldn't figure out his new recruit. He was a smart leader, better than many Haskins had seen in Vietnam. He kept his men in plain sight whenever they camped, so anyone coming at them had to cross open ground; when he traveled, he allowed the men to stretch out in the woods, "to trip an ambush before the main body would walk stupidly into it," he said. Once Haskins got into a conversation with a fellow foot soldier, a man named Quigg. He was from the South Britain countryside and longed to return, but the king had sent them overseas to fight the French, and here he was, dodging the natives, who ran and hid in the trees and fired arrows from anywhere and nowhere at the same time.

"Would you consider deserting?" Haskins asked him.

"To where? Not on your life," Quigg shot back. "To the Indians, them bloody savages? If I am to die, let me die like a man."

"But what's this war about?" Haskins asked him. "What's the king need this land for? And what's in it for you?"

"If the French get this area," Quinn told him, "what's to stop them from taking the whole bloody new world? And then where'll we be? France and Spain, they're all alike, the greedy bastards. It's up to England to stop them. I just want to get it over with and then get back home to me family."

Haskins was thinking how much it all sounded like the twentieth-century "domino theory," which had been used to send him and other American men to Asia. At least the king wasn't trying to say he was preserving democracy for the Indians, he thought. Come to think of it, the English would win this war. What do you know? He smiled.

The major called an end to the break, and the one hundred men, relieved to get moving again, started off. They reached the pass around West Peak, right where Haskins had promised. It followed a narrow creek around several treacherous corners, twisting its way toward a large, open hillside about a mile beyond. The scout, Christoph, went ahead and reported no French but a handful of Indians where the pass reopened on the other side.

"Haskins, you're out front," said Major Gilley. Haskins, Quigg, and three others took the first line, and when they hit the opening on a dead run as the major had ordered, arrows flew out of the trees, landing all around but missing until, wanting a closer target, two Indian braves jumped into the clearing with Tomahawks raised, running right at them. Haskins, thirty paces away, dropped to his stomach and fired, laying the first man flat in his tracks. Quigg shot the other from a kneeling position, and they were through the pass. The entire group followed and regrouped another two miles along the creek, where the hillsides opened into a series of low, rolling hills.

The major sent for Haskins.

"Where did you learn to do that?"

"Vietnam." How could he explain that even England would lose to the settlers of this land, who would then turn around and fight a war against the natives of another?

"Where did you learn this pass through the mountains?"

"I grew up near here. Major, I should tell you something: I know the river's ahead of us, but there are some lakes in between, and I don't know the way."

"That will be Christoph's job, then. Dismissed."

For two days they moved slowly. Finally, on what Haskins guessed to be August 13, they were attacked from the rear, on the shore of the lake that would someday adjoin Middletown. The Indians appeared out of nowhere and disappeared just as quickly into the trees. Two soldiers were killed. Haskins, at the front of the column, did not fire any shots.

On August 17, they reached the Connecticut River. Haskins stood on a hill overlooking the shining water. The last time he'd seen this river, it was black, thick with the slime of the factories, sick with the oil that leaked in a steady stream from the small boats that navigated it, and dark with the sewage of towns and cities from Springfield through Hartford through Middletown. And what had enriched the manufacturers and the politicians had been taken out of this beautiful river, which now danced in the midday sun, full of fish, full of life, full of pride. And it made him wish the English lost this war so his own son could someday see this water shine.

My own son? he caught himself. What an idea.

Christoph said there was a fort two miles to the south. They started downriver, and at the first bend, they saw the French. And suddenly, they were all grouped in rows, powder in the muskets, and Haskins was kneeling in the front row, waiting for the signal to fire. Seconds later, it came as smoke rose from the blue uniforms fifty yards away. All around him, the men were falling. Haskins fired, and after hitting no one, he dove backward into the forest of soldiers' boots, crawling to the rear for more powder and shot.

"Haskins," the major called.

"Yes, sir."

"Do we win this battle?"

"I don't know, sir."

"Have you hit anyone yet?"

"No, sir."

He drew a quick drink of water from the leather flask he wore across his stomach, and when he looked down, something whizzed past his ear and hit nearby with a thud. Gilley was kneeling, spitting blood.

"Major! Are you hit?"

Gilley reached up, grabbed the collar of Rett's uniform, and pulled him down to the ground. He was much stronger than Haskins, and he held them in his arms as together they fell, the major dying, the recruit unhurt.

"Here. When the shots have all been fired, they will come," the major wheezed, "and search you. To the south is the sea." He shoved the small box of matches into Rett's hand.

After a while, the firing stopped. Face down, hammerlocked under the dead man, he closed his eyes when the first French soldier kicked a body nearby, went through his pockets, and found nothing. A foot slammed into his side, and he held his breath, clenching his fists and pressing his face into the ground as Gilley's grip slid away. He closed his eyes and lay there, keeping still, breathing as quietly as possible amid the stench of gunpowder and blood.

When he opened his eyes, it was nearly dark. He looked everywhere he could without moving his head. There seemed to be no one around except the corpses of the dead soldiers. He moved his head slightly, slowly, until he had seen in every direction. But the living had abandoned the area. He crawled out from under Gilley's body, still half sprawled across his back, and stood up.

The English had been routed. Their slain bodies were strewn across the field, sprawled in every conceivable position. The French had collected all the muskets. Gilley had found the river, and his death, his last bequest a small wooden matchbox that opened at each end with several stick matches inside.

There was a campfire in the distance, down the river, and he walked stealthily around it, carving a wide arc south, until he reached the banks of the river again. The sun would rise soon, and he found a thicket of underbrush, where he hid himself carefully and slept. He traveled by night, keeping the river at his side, ate wild blueberries that grew freely above the banks, and, as the sun rose on the next day, reached the mouth of the river. The smell of saltwater rose before him; he kept going until he reached the open sea. The sun was low; he needed sleep, and he found a spot in the nearby woods where he could see the ocean.

When he awoke, he crossed the pebble-strewn beach to the waterline and started digging, his hands tearing up chunks of muddy water. He found the clams a foot down, two to three inches long, their black tails sticking out of orange-circled shells, and piled them on the beach. He found dried grass, twigs and pieces of wood, opened the matchbox, and built a small fire, roasting all the clams he could eat. He kept the fire going, sleeping in snatches and eating clams and blackberries from the seaside underbrush. He assembled a small hut from driftwood, sheltering the fire and himself from a late August thunderstorm. Huddled inside, he found the joint, unfound in the recess of his pocket; he lit it and took a long toke, then drifted off into thought as he watched the fire. Intermittently lighting it and staring, unmoving, at the quiet flames, he smoked it all the way down and eventually fell asleep. He dreamed of an airplane, but when he awoke, the air was as still as always, save for the birds, the insects, and the surf. The fire was still alive, and he fed it some twigs and watched the ocean, its ceaseless rising and falling, until he heard footsteps and voices over the dunes, and knew his night on the mountain had ended: The Indians had come for him. He sat facing the sea until two tall men walked in front of him, wearing uniforms and handguns.

They were the Connecticut State Police.

The
American
Guerrillas

Chapter 1

——◦◦◦——

"I DON'T KNOW WHAT TO MAKE OF HIM, SIR," THE CLERK OF THE station office was telling the captain, a short, round man with a short, fat, black cigar stuck slantedly into his lips. "No papers, no license, no identifying labels in his clothes, no watch, and he won't give us a name. And the reporters want to know if we've caught a suspect; we can't give them this one, we don't even know who he is."

"Well, Crandall, let's wait him out. Has he contacted anyone?"

"No, sir."

"Let me know if he does. In fact, offer him a phone call."

Crandall went to the cell at the end of the concrete hallway and woke up the sleeping beach bum. Those funny clothes, he was thinking. These homeless people will wear anything.

"The captain says you're entitled to a phone call."

The prisoner followed the clerk down the corridor. He did not look for an escape; he didn't even know why he was there but had sensed from the first sight of the state troopers that his own odyssey had only begun and its course wouldn't be up to him for some time. He had not spoken a word to any of these people; he went with them in body but gave them nothing of his mind or identity. His fingerprints, if they existed at all, were mired deep in the military, and if known to state police here, he did not explain why he would not tell anyone who he was.

"Is there a legal aid lawyer in this town?" were his first and only words. They were required to say, "Yes."

"Good. Dial him." His voice, the sound of it, reverberated in the clerk's ears a moment; it was a perfectly sane, normal voice, not the shrill, fearful sound of a maniac.

An hour later, the lawyer arrived and was escorted to the cell.

"My name is Irby Braxton," said the young, well-suited, and long-haired man with the man-about-campus grin. "What's yours?"

"First things first," replied the prisoner. Standing up, his pants a somewhat faded blue, visibly torn at his right knee, he spoke quietly.

"I don't know why I'm here or where here is. Can you fill me in?"

"All I know is you were picked up on the beach and won't tell anyone your name."

"I don't know."

"Your name? You don't know who you are?"

He shook his head.

"So. You were picked up on the beach, a vagrant. Officially, there is no charge against you yet. But around here, they don't take well to living on the beach with no money."

"Why's that?"

The lawyer laughed.

"What are you, some kind of fool? It won't work."

"That's what you can call me. Fool."

The lawyer frowned, serious.

"Well. The real reason you're here is for questioning. It seems there's been a murder a few miles up the river, and a man was seen running away, described as dressed strangely, red coat with military buttons, like something from a hippie thrift shop. They found the coat a few miles up the river. The rest of the description matches you."

"A murder?" murmured the fool, shaking his head.

"Who was killed?"

"A narcotics investigator, a high-ranking one. Name of Giles. Seems he was onto some smuggling operation, a small boat landing upriver posing as a fishing party. You can imagine they are out to get the man who did it. They suspect it's you."

The lawyer's eyes widened as he finished. He caught his breath, nearly doubled over, and went on.

"Anything you want to tell me about it?"

Rett sat on his bunk.

"Giles? Never heard of a Giles. I wasn't smuggling anything. I was just sleeping on the beach."

"Can you tell me what you were doing before that?"

He shook his head.

"No. I can't."

Irby Braxton closed his briefcase and watched him through the bars.

"I see," he said. "Well, until they get some answers, you can expect to be here a while. They won't release you."

"Where am I?"

"This is the Old Lyme State Police headquarters. You were picked up a few miles away, day before yesterday. You've got real problems. You should tell me anything you can remember. The papers are on a crusade to clean up smuggling traffic, and they'd love to throw you to the lions. Were you involved in this?"

"No." He stared straight into his eyes. Irby Braxton blinked and stepped back.

"Well, I had to ask." He shook his head. "You know, I believe you. What do you want me to do?"

"Can you speak to the papers?"

"The papers? There's a battalion of them outside, TV, radio, even network news."

"Tell them this: the Fool remembers Jimmy with love and sends him a rodeo."

"What is that supposed to mean?"

"It doesn't matter. Repeat it to me."

"The Fool sends Jimmy his love and a rodeo."

"The Fool remembers Jimmy with love and sends him a rodeo." He made him repeat it, slowly this time, until it was right.

⚘

For two days, the telephone rang in the empty Chicago apartment. Lina moved out, following the advice of her manager, who said her modeling career would improve if she weren't so closely tied to the seldom-published writer she slept and sometimes lived with. The only problem was, she still missed him, and was back at his apartment, picking up some clothes she always left behind. The telephone rang again.

"Hello."

"Lina?"

"Yes."

"You don't know me, but Rett told me about you. Is he there?"

"No." She hesitated. "We had an argument, and he took a drive for a few days."

"Where?"

"He said something about New England. He even mentioned seeing the old place in Connecticut. Who is this?"

But the phone was already dead.

⚘

"You're being arraigned next Tuesday," the guard told him on Friday morning. "Until then, you're going to have a cellmate."

"Will I be going to court?" he asked.

"Yes."

"Then there's something I want. No pictures. I don't want to be bothered by people for the rest of my life when this is over."

"This may never be over for you, pal," said the guard, "but if it's no pictures, cover your face between the car and the court, and you're okay. No cameras are allowed inside."

∽

Four fishermen sitting in a shack near the Rhode Island coast went over the paper. *The New York Post* had smeared the headlines in type so large the edition was famous along the entire Eastern Seaboard—and the "Fool With No Name" was a household word from Maine to Florida.

"You should never had shot him, Lake."

"It was him or us. He wanted too much for a share, got too greedy."

"Lake's right," said a third man. "But the real question is, what do we do about this other guy?"

"Why do anything?" said Lake. The first man hung his head. Here he was, making some money and collecting stories for a book, and now he's an accessory to murder. He turned to the others.

"Look, we know Giles was a scumbag, but this guy is just some loony who was in the wrong place at the wrong time. Why don't we spring him?"

"Are you nuts? Go back there? This whole thing could be a setup."

"I say we waylay the car on its way to court."

"Too risky. But I agree," said the fourth man, a burly quiet presence in a baseball cap and sunglasses. "Let's spring him before the trial, right out of the jailhouse. It's just a state police barracks, minimal security, nobody would expect."

"And they're right," declared Lake. "You guys are nuts. I'm leaving."

"Lake. You're forgetting something. The dope is still on the boat. No one splits until we move it."

Lake exhaled and stood up, speaking quietly.

"All right. You guys get the nut out of jail. I've gotta go."

∽

Though the general public had no idea what the Fool looked like, his police identification photo went everywhere. It met no response until it hit the desk of Bill Scanlon, one of dozens of photographs a week to cross his desk at the Federal Bureau of Investigation. There was no mistaking this face, for though it belonged to no police file anywhere, it had lived inside Scanlon's head for six years, since the day his ex-wife had shown it to him and said he was the father of her son, born seven months after they were married. And although he had tried to hold the wife and be a father to the son, he was not the father, and he had failed. He picked up the telephone to call Florida.

A minute passed. This would be hard.

"Bill. What's the occasion?"

"Linda, I've just come across a photograph of the man you told me is Timmy's father."

"What?"

"Have you heard of the Fool up in Connecticut?"

"The smuggler who killed a cop? Come on, Bill."

"It's him, Linda. I'm going up to see him."

"Don't you dare tell him where I am."

"I'll decide that after I see him. But, Linda, I need his name."

There was a prolonged silence.

"Forget it."

"Linda, I need his name. This is a federal investigation."

"And I said no. No. Period. No."

Scanlon tried another tack.

"How's Timmy these days?"

"You know damn well how he is. The doctors say he's in remission, and they say that can last two days or a lifetime. I bite my nails."

"Linda, I need his name. Now."

"You goddamn bastard, if Timmy had a decent father around the house, he wouldn't be like this. Twelve years old, and he might die any time, and you're still playing cops and robbers. Fuck off."

"I'll find out, one way or the other. I'll find out."

But she was already gone.

⌘

"Tell them this: the Fool remembers Jimmy with love and sends him a rodeo." It had to be Rett, thought Quisto. Who else would say that? Why was Rett accused of smuggling and murder? He did something he had never done before: he lied to his wife.

"I'm going fishing for a couple of days with the guys. You have anything planned for the weekend?"

"Nothing special," she said. "Is anything wrong?"

"Nope, nothing's wrong. You don't mind, do you?"

She let it go. He was moody sometimes since their boy had been lost, spending time alone and with his card-playing friends. But it didn't make sense to be suspicious or worry about other women. She didn't think he was like that.

On Friday afternoon, Quisto left New Jersey for Old Lyme, Connecticut, a spot on the map. He had taken a week's vacation just in case, and as he walked to the car, his wife laughed and said, "Don't get mixed up with any smugglers while you're fishing."

He shuddered and stepped on the gas.

Chapter 2

——⟊⟊⟊——

"AN OLD MAN IS STANDING ON A SNOW-COVERED PEAK. IN HIS right hand, he holds a lantern with a bright, shining star inside it. In his left, he holds a staff. In his eyes is the wisdom of insight into humanity, wise, perhaps a little sad but not bitter."

He folded up the deck and put it back in a small box.

Haskins looked across the cell at his new mate. The other man wore a simple loose-fitting sweatshirt and yoga pants. He had white hair fanning out in random directions from the top of his head and a thin white goatee. The man could be a plant, working for the police, and Rett was not going to tell him anything. But he wasn't opposed to learning something or having someone to talk with.

"What is that you're doing?" he asked. The old man, who had introduced himself as Geller, shrugged.

"Tarot cards," he replied. "They tell me what's going and coming beyond these walls. Want to try it?"

Haskins walked across the cell and sat down. He took the cards and did as Geller told him, shuffling them, turning them around, and finally handing them back. Geller cut them three times and dealt them out: two in the center, a circle around them, then a straight line of four cards on the side. He began turning them over.

"Queen of Cups. One's romance dreams and one's reality meet. An auspicious start." He turned over another.

"Five of Cups. Your life is in your own hands. Hardly seems that way, ay? See the cups, how they're overturned? Notice only the contents are lost, the cups are not broken. They can always be refilled.

"Let's see, your past history, the judgment, a big card. Your life is winding up a cycle or beginning one now, my friend. As you reap, ye shall sow. The need to take a long look at yourself, where you're going, my friend."

"The present. Eight of Pentacles. Hmm. You don't look like someone who's got money stashed away or is working hard enough to be planning on it."

"Now wait a minute."

"Don't get steamed up. Perhaps it means you're someone who's been learning the ability to provide for himself. You'd be amazed how few people know that. What were you living on before you came to this place?"

"I was digging clams."

Geller laughed so hard his leg shot out and knocked over the cards. "Digging clams. I might've known. I should've known." Geller stroked his goatee once, then started picking up the cards.

"Well, back to your immediate future," he said, turning over a new card. It was III, the High Priestess. They stared at it, sitting on Geller's knee: a woman seated, a horned crown on her head. When the fool looked up, he met the older man's eyes and shivered.

"A very strong card, my friend. An essential step in the rites of passage from innocence to wisdom, this woman; she represents the unbroken chain of ancient knowledge, the knowledge of magic and harmony, which can only be passed on to an initiate in such matters, one wise enough to live within it."

"Wait a minute. Are you saying I'm to meet someone like this?"

"Perhaps," said Geller. "But the card has a fuller meaning: all the wisdom and magic one ever needs is contained within one's own will and subconscious. Your inner wisdom is the key; the priestess is the teacher to show you how to use that energy. Let's move on."

The next card was the Queen of Swords. Geller called it the future outcome of the immediate cycle.

"A very interesting card, this one. This card probably does and also doesn't pertain directly to you. Its general meaning is that one has to go it alone. But its feminine gender also indicates that in the future for you is a woman who has had to defend her own life and position unaided by the man who would be her king. This is a widow's card, a divorced woman's card. For you, it is also a lonely but strong place."

Geller told Haskins he would read four more cards, explaining he followed a traditional route. Rett drew again.

"The place you are in with the world is next. Nine of Wands. Again a prosperous card. Something you are not aware of is making you wealthy, perhaps. Either that or you can take a spiritualist interpretation."

"Such as?"

"Your spirit, your soul, my friend. Your spirit is rapidly becoming enriched from experience, and my guess is that it spent a long time in its dormant state." He turned over a new card.

"This card is your environment. The King of Cups." Geller stopped.

"What is it?"

"This card is very powerful. In your environment is a man who's a swami, a guru, big brother, teacher, whose throne rests on the water that is the river of the unconscious. See the throne? It symbolizes someone who will teach you the threads that tie your power together."

He drew again. On the card were eight cups in the foreground, but the figure of a man was walking away, slightly hunched and leaning on a staff, as if he were shrugging off the contents of the cups.

"Your inner desires, my friend. For all that you find, you search for more, for higher things. You will, again and again, abandon the cups to learn the secrets of the mountains in the distance."

Rett, beginning to feel tired, found the man's soothing voice and fiery eyes to be hypnotic. Geller took the last card and held it out face down.

"All right, then. This card will be you, the end product of the influences we have examined. Are you ready to see it?"

The Fool nodded. Geller turned it over, setting it on his knee at the apex of the wheel of cards.

It was the magician.

When he looked up, Geller was staring into his eyes with a light that burned like none he had ever seen. The old man moved his hand in a small circle, drawing the younger man's glance into it, entranced, until Rett's eyelids grew heavy and closed.

"Can you hear me?" Geller whispered.

"Yes."

"Are you ready to answer my questions?"

"Yes."

"Are you from the police?"

"No."

"Why are you here?"

"I was living on the beach."

"And before?"

"I was a ..."

He stopped speaking and shook his head as if shaking loose an answer embedded deep inside.

"Soldier," he said at last, inhaling a large gulp of air.

"US military? Vietnam?"

"Yes. Vietnam."

"And since then?"

He shook his head again.

"British."

"Where? What unit?"

He was shaking, compelled to provide answers he could not understand.

"French and Indian War," he got out, exhaling heavily.

Geller, still balancing the cards on his leg, leaned against the wall.

"Where? What year?"

"Connecticut. 1762."

"How did you get to the beach?"

"I ran."

"When?"

"From a battle. All killed."

Geller took a breath and considered his next question.

"You say you are here from 1762?"

"I was there."

"From here."

"Yes."

The old man studied his cellmate. No one ever lied to him under hypnosis.

"Do you know who I am?"

"No."

"Did you come here to get information for the FBI?"

"No."

Gellar looked slowly around the spare cell.

"What's your name?" he continued.

"Rett Haskins," the Fool replied slowly.

"Is it true you've been to 1762. And back. Through time?"

"I … think so."

"How did it happen?"

"I walked into the woods."

Geller looked at the card on his knee, the one that described the future of the questioner. And it was The Magician.

"Hear me," he said. "We haven't much time. I'm far older than you realize. You must give me all your concentrated energies. You must learn to master your will. Do you understand?"

"Yes," Rett whispered hoarsely.

"Do you want me to teach you?"

"Yes," came the soft reply.

Geller nodded, as if to himself, for now he understood. He looked at the cell window, high on the wall; the daylight was fading, and he wondered if he would ever feel the sun on his body again. But he was without remorse, for now he had one more task: to pass on his lifetime's knowledge.

"Good. Give me your hands."

Haskins held them up, palms down. Geller took them gently, examining the soft creases on the back, then turning them over.

"Your lifeline is strong," he said. "Your heart must be stronger." He ran his fingernails across the palm as if he were sketching a line.

"You will have a new life when you awaken," he spoke quietly. "As a magician. Is this your wish?"

The head nodded now, up and down.

"Yes," the voice whispered.

"Very well. You will awaken now. And you will remember."

Rett sat up and opened his eyes, blinking twice as if returning from a long ways off. He looked up to see a whitehaired man sitting there, the picture cards spread across his leg like a trail of footprints. He rubbed his eyes.

"What was the last card again?" he asked.

"It's your future," said the old magician. He took a hand-rolled cigarette from his shirt pocket and lit it with his last match, leaning into the cold concrete wall as he let out the smoke.

Throughout the weekend, Rett listened to the quiet, soothing voice. Meals came and went uneaten; the daytime, interrupted only by a thirty-minute walk in the enclosed yard, passed unnoticed into night. It was late Sunday evening as he sat against the wall.

"This life has four elements," said Geller. "There are earth, air, water, and fire. They are the basis of all things in this life. Even the buildings are made from the minerals of earth, heated until they turn to liquid, and poured to stand in the air and harden."

"And so are you. You stand on the earth and will return to the earth. You are mostly water, yet you cannot last without air. And inside all that is your fire, the fire of life that binds you together into a living, conscious being. And behind that flame, beyond all anger and desire, sadness and need, is your essence, the place that is one with Creation. From that essence flows your power, aware that Creation is everlasting and is always occurring. It is a state of true grace, one that cannot be purchased with prayers or donations. When that essence surfaces in you, you have power."

Geller paused and waited for it to sink in. Rett sat on the floor and waited back. It seemed he had not spoken in hours.

"Are you there?"

"Yes, I'm listening."

"But are you learning anything?"

"Well, you haven't taught me to do anything."

"Do anything? Like what?"

"Like, what was it, deflect an action? Isn't that what you called it? What am I supposed to do with all this information?"

Geller stiffened a moment, then relaxed into a smile.

"I'm just trying to tell you some things. But you're right—it's only words unless you figure out how to use it." And he sat down on his bunk, kicking off his shoes.

"Are you going to teach me that, too?"

The older man lay back and stretched.

"That comes with a need for that kind of ability. The thing is to be genuinely and spontaneously acting from your real self, emotions and all, and still acting with consciousness of your power. Otherwise, it happens to you, by itself, if you have a gift. Take your walk into the woods. That was real magic."

Rett sighed heavily as if remembering a repressed secret.

"You certainly looked inside my head," he said.

"Your head? Your life. That happened to you from need, the need to start again. It left you open to something like that."

"Something like what? I still don't understand it. How is it possible I traveled through time?"

"Why not? On the deepest level, you create your own perception of time, according to need. Just as you create all your perceptions, at such a profound level you're consciously unaware of it. If the need changed, and you were where free-floating perceptions could find you, why not?"

Rett got up and paced around.

"You know, there are men who get in the car one day and drive off, leaving a wife, kids, job, house, everything. And they never go back, as if they realize they're on the other side ... of something."

"Yes, that's true. But they only moved to a different place on the planet. You traveled in time—physical time, you say—yet you don't believe it yourself."

"How can I? Do you believe it? That I walked in and out of a different time because I needed to start a new life?"

"Yes," said Geller. "It's why I'm teaching you."

The single bulb in the ceiling went off.

"Lights out," a voice called.

"I sure am doing great so far," Rett said, kicking off his shoes.

"Well, you have to start somewhere," Geller observed, "but I don't hear you wishing to go back to your old life, do I?"

"No," he replied, stretching out on the bunk. "All right, then, can you teach me to travel through time when and where I want?"

"Why don't you try this instead for now? Imagine an object is moving through a scene, and you slow the scene down around the object, so you and it are moving in one energy, and everything else, more slowly."

Rett stared into the lightless room.

"It's hard to imagine."

"It's up to you."

"You know," the younger man spoke into the darkness, "you never even said why you're here."

"I chained myself to a nuclear submarine."

Rett laughed slowly.

"You're really a menace to society," he whispered. "So, that's why you thought I was from the FBI?"

"It happens."

"Could you prevent me from remembering something?"

"I could tell your conscious mind to ignore it. But sooner or later, the subconscious would let it out."

"I understand. But why me? Why not someone else?"

"Oh, there are others. I can only tell you there is an unbroken line. It was given to me a long time ago, and now I see you as the person who's come for this knowledge, which is a sacred thing. You may develop some of my abilities, without even knowing what or why, because the line must continue. So pay attention. This is something that has been passed down for thousands, maybe millions, of years, and is treasured now by a tiny number. And now you. Treat it with reverence."

"There are others?"

"Of course. You will know them. But you've learned too much, too quickly, for now. You have to give yourself some time to learn what to do."

"Like time traveling?"

"Anything's possible."

"Meanwhile, they think I killed somebody. I can't even explain what happened myself."

"Don't try," returned Geller. "If it could be explained, it wouldn't be magic."

The apprentice lay in the dark, wide awake.

"So, you mean magic is what you can't explain?"

There was no answer from the other side of the cell. He waited, and the quiet of the police unit seeped into the room. Like an unwanted visitor, it moved around the space, sampling various places to sit down and stay. In response, Geller's breathing broke into a cyclical pattern of round, baritone inhalations and soft whistles, driving the intruding silence out with his snores. But after some minutes, he turned on his side, and the apprentice was left to stare into the empty, soundless dark until, much later, he fell asleep.

Chapter 3

———◦◦◦———

H E SAW QUISTO SITTING IN THE CORNER OF THE COURTROOM AS HE walked in. The room was crowded, as befitted the well-publicized trial, but Jim was staring at the entrance and gasped. Rett looked his way; he shook his head slightly, his eyes giving away nothing, and hoped the message arrived. Then he took a seat.

The first thing he discovered was he had a new lawyer. She took his hand and smiled.

"Your attorney has been reassigned. I'll be handling your case. My name is Rosalie Lenoir, spelled L-E-N-O-I-R. I have what your lawyer wrote, which isn't much. Is there anything you want me to be aware of?"

"Not especially."

"They'll want you to plead. I assume you're pleading not guilty."

He took a long breath.

"Yes," he said. "Is that what you advise?"

She studied his eyes for a long moment, looked right into them, and smiled again.

"Well, let's see what they have to say."

The judge entered, and everyone stood, then sat down, except his lawyer. She was primly tucked into a skirt and jacket, looking as if she would be pretty if she untied the hair pulled severely back behind her. It was long, red hair; he had always liked long red hair, and as he watched her move around, to the bench for a conference with the judge and prosecutor, then back across the room, he wished she would untie it. He started to laugh at himself.

"It's time to stand up, Mr. Fool."

She turned around, faced the judge, and nodded.

"How does the defendant plead?" came the voice from the bench, a deep, authoritative sound that quieted the constant rustle of clothing and paper in the courtroom.

"Not guilty, Your Honor," he said.

The judge, a middle-aged man with the cropped haircut of an army sergeant, nodded blankly and said, "November 6." He shrugged, pounded the gavel, and stood up. Everyone rose. Seconds later, there was bedlam as reporters yelled questions from the gallery toward the famous unseen face; four silent men sat at the back of the room and sized him up.

From his corner, Quisto saw the three other men across the back row; when everyone else was standing, trying to get to Rett, they remained seated, watching. In seconds, the defendant was gone, back to the van transporting him to his cell. They got up and left, and Quisto followed, curious to know why they were there. Three miles outside town, they pulled into a diner. Quisto parked his car and went in also; he spotted the empty booth behind them and sat in it.

"I know he can't risk being seen by that witness, but it pisses me off having to mop up for him again just because he's trigger-happy."

"Listen, forget that. We gotta spring this guy. He's got no reason to be there."

"You're both off base," said a third voice. "Okay, he didn't do it, but it'll take months before they find out. Meantimes, we get the load and get out of here."

"What if they nail him for it?"

"What if they do? I mean, is that what's important right now?"

There was a silence.

"It just isn't right," said the first voice.

"What, you got morals? All right, if it starts looking bad, we'll pay somebody to spring him down the line. He can disappear, and no one will ever know."

Quisto looked up, and the waiter was standing there.

"Coffee," he said. "Black."

"If all you want's coffee, sir, please sit at the counter."

The next booth got quiet.

"Bring me a sandwich. Tuna salad. Oh, and ask these gentlemen if I may join them."

The waiter raised his eyebrows, but finishing writing on his pad, took a step to his right and repeated the request to the next booth. He walked away without waiting for an answer.

Three hard faces looked into his eyes as he slid into their booth.

"I'll spring him if you'll get him out of here," he said.

✑

When they returned him to his cell, he found to his dismay that Geller was gone; in his place was a middle-aged man with thinning brown hair, wearing clean pants and a shirt.

"Where's the old man?" he asked the guard. The guard looked at him for a moment, then shrugged, looked away, and closed the cell door, answering through the bars.

"Dead," he said. "Heart attack, this morning."

Rett planted his feet, leaned against the wall, and exhaled.

Across the cell, the new man rolled over toward him. He swung his legs to the floor, stood up, and walked toward Rett, extending a hand.

"Name's Scanlon," he said. "How about you?"

He didn't answer; after a few seconds, the man went to his bunk and sat down.

"Not very friendly of you," said Scanlon.

"I'm not your friend. Please leave me alone." He stretched out on the bunk and was drifting off when the guard walked up to their door.

"Your lawyer's here. Good looker. Wants to see you. You want to come to the conference room?"

"Why don't you just show her in here?"

The guard looked over at Scanlon and said, "Sure, why not?"

Rosalie Lenoir entered a few seconds later, looking very different than in court: she wore a loose-fitting white blouse with embroidered edges and a long peasant skirt of red and blue cotton. She looked stunning, with her fine cheekbones, smooth skin, and bright blue eyes framed by the long red hair that hung, full and rich, around her shoulders. The only flaw in her beauty was in her eyes, where a trace of red betrayed that she had been crying.

"I was on my way home. You don't mind?"

"No." Scanlon lay on his bunk, his back to them. She sat next to him on his.

"Why won't you tell anyone your name?"

"I don't wish anyone to know who I am."

"Are you someone?"

"Everyone is someone."

"Are you someone dangerous?" she asked quietly. "Should I be afraid of you?"

"No, you shouldn't be afraid of me," he replied.

"Okay. But how can I defend you if you won't open up to me?"

"I can't help you there."

"All right. Did you do it?"

"No," he said.

"You're a very strange man, Mr. Fool. Can you tell me where you were the night they say you killed this man?"

"I was along the banks of the river, walking south. But I met no one, no one at all."

"Do you remember any specific points of the riverbank? Do you know the area? Are there any places you were that would be too far away from the killing to have allowed you to be there?"

"I don't know."

He glanced at Scanlon again. As if understanding, she looked at Scanlon too; perhaps he was listening, pretending to be sleeping. But the silence was abruptly broken by a whisper from the window.

"Front gate," it said.

A hard metal object flew in and clacked on the floor. Scanlon rose immediately from his cot, diving toward the sound, but as if he slowed down in midair, he arrived too late, as Rett kicked the pistol clear and shoved Scanlon back toward his bunk, where he whacked hard against the wall and went down. Footsteps were approaching in the corridor. He picked up the pistol and crossed the room to Rosalie.

"Kiss me," he said.

"What?"

"Kiss me," he repeated. He grabbed her long dress in his hand and raised it up, sliding his gun hand underneath along her leg, his fingers between the cold metal and her skin, until he reached her underclothes. He pushed the pistol under her panties, and she gasped; they were kissing as the guard arrived.

"What's the ruckus?"

Rosalie pointed at Scanlon, sitting with his back against the wall, his eyes closed.

"It's all right, officer. That man attacked me, but everything is under control now."

The guard looked very confused.

"Maybe you could get some water and we could bring him around," she continued. The guard left, locking the door behind him.

The prisoner stood eyeing his lawyer. She didn't move either of the hands on her hips.

"What are you going to do?" she finally asked, tilting her head slightly to the side. He moved in front of her again, taking the dress in his hand, slowly, carefully not touching her skin, until his fingers felt like feathers and he moved his hand over her hip and caressed her stomach, until she let him take his hand down over her navel and down to the gun.

The guard was back with a bucket of water. Rett drew out the gun and stepped away from her. The guard's eyes got wide.

"Throw it in his face," he ordered. The guard did it. Scanlon moaned and began to sit up slowly.

"Now, put your gun on the floor, sit in the corner, and be quiet." Rett watched him sit in the corner and turned to Scanlon.

"All right, who are you? Why are you here?" But the man was still in a daze. Rett put the gun barrel against his cheek.

"One more time," he said.

"I'm your son's father. Well, stepfather. Linda Terrazzo was my wife. She had a baby. Your baby. His name's Timmy."

Rett reeled back, stunned. He drew away, and Scanlon began coming around.

"Do you know this man's name?" Rosalie cut in.

"Yes."

"How did you find me here?"

"The FBI has all ID photos. It's routine. I spotted yours because it matched one Linda had."

"You're FBI?"

"Yes." The voice answered faintly.

It began to hit him. The way she had looked when he said goodbye; she must have known even then.

"Where's Linda now?"

"Florida."

"Where?"

"I told her I wouldn't tell you."

He looked hard into Scanlon's eyes.

"Where is she?"

"Lantana."

Rosalie interrupted nervously.

"Is this true? Do you know this person?"

"What's my name?" he continued on the agent, ignoring her.

"Haskins. Rett Haskins."

He stood up. Rosalie was standing behind him, her arms across her chest, a worried look in her eyes. He led her to his cot and sat her down, then waved the guard to slide across the floor to where Scanlon sat, as if entranced. He stared deeply into the guard's eyes, then into Scanlon's, until he felt each go quiet.

"You will not awaken until someone walks in here and says your names," he told them, watching them slip to the floor. He went back to the cot.

"Okay," he said. "Time to go."

"What about me?"

"I'm afraid you're coming. Are you all right?"

"Yes. I'm all right. And I won't be any trouble. But why are you doing this? If you didn't do it?"

"I didn't do it. But you'd never convince anybody of that."

The corridor was empty, and the only guard at the entrance was reading the newspaper. They snuck past him to a gate, where another officer leaned back in a chair, a rifle leaning against the wall. A revolving beacon punctuated the darkness; they waited until it passed, then tapped the wall. The guard stood up.

"Who's there?"

Seconds passed. The guard came down carefully.

Rosalie stepped forward. "I'm trying to get out to my car. I was visiting a client." She smiled, and the guard was entranced. He opened the gate, and Rett stepped up from behind, pressing the gun into his side.

"Keep going. Don't move."

A car was waiting outside. They took the guard with them in the back seat, face down. Down the road, in an abandoned area, they dumped him out, unharmed.

James Quisto turned around and smiled.

The fugitive smiled back.

"Thanks for coming, buddy."

There was no one at the small airstrip, and no one saw the small plane buzz out low over the water. Rett and Rosalie were silently handed parachutes, then shoved out an open hatchway over some small lights in the dark water. They hit the cold, wet sea, and the boat pulled up; three men helped the two exhausted, shivering swimmers into the small craft.

They were shown to a small room in the hull, where he insisted on taking care of her himself. She was murmuring drowsily, incoherently, as he peeled off her skirt and blouse and undergarments and hung them up on a makeshift line, soaking wet. He put her to bed, stripped and crawled in under the covers, and passed out.

In the night, he had a dream: he was home again, home in South Airville, playing baseball. This time, the field swayed back and forth, and the players had no faces. Each time Rett came up to bat, he hit the ball between two players and ran to first base. But each time, the first-base umpire stepped up and said, "I'm sorry, but you're not allowed to hit the ball there. You have to go back." He said it over and over, each time in the same monotone, no matter where Rett hit the ball. Finally the umpire ripped off the mask and exposed, behind his blank face, the face of Major Gilley. All the players fell down, and Rett woke up.

There was a thin gray light coming in the porthole. It was just before dawn. Somehow Rosalie had rested her head on his shoulder, and he had his arm around her. She stirred slightly, and slowly, she woke up.

"Where are we?"

"We're on a ship, I suppose. We're safe, probably. Are you all right?"

She half-turned and looked into his eyes.

"Yes, I think so," she said.

He put his arm around her waist and drew her toward him. She brought her face down and kissed him, slowly opening her mouth until they were kissing passionately. She straddled him, and they rolled over, him lying between her legs. It was as if, in his whole life, he had never wanted a woman more than he wanted Rosalie; her skin and body glowed in his arms as he held her, as she embraced him with her legs. Holding her light frame up, he rose to his knees until she was completely suspended in midair, her arms around his neck, her legs around his waist.

When he woke again, Rosalie was still asleep. He got up and dressed and went on deck. They were beyond sight of land and seemed to be heading south, the sun behind them. Three men came over in sunglasses and hats.

"So," one said, "you're the cop killer. Sleep okay?"

"Yes, thank you. Who are you, and why am I here? In fact, where are we?"

"You're in the Atlantic. We worked a deal with your friend—that's all you need to know. Except one thing: you owe us a favor now."

"What sort of favor?"

"This whole thing started over a cargo. The cargo's on this boat. You're going to take it to shore."

He stood there and knew better than to ask what kind of cargo.

"Well. Where?"

"Florida."

The boat rose and fell beneath their feet as he thought it over.

"What if I don't want to get involved in this?"

The three men exchanged glances through the opaque lenses on their eyes. The one in the middle looked out over the blue water, stretching from one horizon to the other, then turned back to Rett.

"Well," he said. "I think you gotta be realistic."

Chapter 4

———◦◦◦———

SOME MORNINGS LATER, THE FISHING VACATIONERS CROSSED THE point off the Florida coast known to be patrolled by special anti-smuggling boats, armed and equipped to board and search all other vessels for drugs. The condition of the waters was bright, blue, and calm, beneath a clear sky and a bright sun. For days, he had done almost nothing but lie in the sun, fish, and make love with Rosalie. They had kept to themselves; he had been careful to ask nothing of these men, and in turn, they had asked nothing of him. He caught some medium-sized fish, cooked one on the small stove inside, and shared the rest. They ate separately and stayed apart from their hosts. She overheard one of them say, "Well, you gotta be realistic," as the other two laughed.

They took him into a compartment, two men standing there in hats, beards, and sunglasses.

"Here's one thousand dollars, a credit card, and driver's licenses. Your name is Dylan Reed. Hers is Jane DeLours. It'll be reported in a few days, so make the most of it. We're putting you off at a place above Jupiter Inlet. There's a small fishermen's motel there. Call this number and tell them who you are." He handed him a slip of paper.

"Take this suitcase with you. Don't open it. Drive to the bus station in West Palm Beach. Put the case in a locker, go into the men's room, and wait until you are alone. Tape the key behind the toilet in the farthest stall. Then take a bus north and disappear."

❦

It had been hours before the next shift came on duty, finding no one at the front wall and the desk guard asleep. Crandall walked into the Fool's cell and found the night guard and Scanlon sitting on the floor, their eyes wide open.

"Jackson!" he exclaimed, and the night guard blinked, stood up, and looked around.

"Where's the Fool?" asked Crandall.

"I don't know. Gone. I don't know," Jackson said, and burst into tears.

Through the day, Scanlon continued staring straight ahead. No one spoke his name, for he had not told it to anyone at the unit; he had called from Washington, persuaded a nearby prison warden to tell the unit that a prisoner would arrive to room with the Fool. He had taken vacation time, flown to Providence, and driven to Old Lyme, and using a fake name, he had not been fingerprinted or identified when he arrived. The state police declared the cell a crime scene and left Scanlon there, brought Scanlon his food three times a day, and watched him eat in silent, robotic movements.

Crandall spoke up.

"Captain, sir."

"What is it?"

"Why don't we fingerprint the guy?"

"Who?"

"The zombie in the cell."

"Crandall, I told you, the federal government, for reasons we aren't to know, doesn't want us to know who he is. But they know who he is."

Crandall was unconvinced.

"Suppose no one knows he's here?" he asked again.

❦

They checked into the inlet motel. There was a phone on the wall by the office, and it cost Rett $1.65 to call the number.

"This is Reed," he said, using his new alias. "I would like to meet you."

"Friday at 2:00 p.m." The phone went dead.

It was a Wednesday, he discovered by buying the paper. He realized he'd long ago lost interest and barely glanced at it. He asked for the phone book and called a local car rental company, which agreed to deliver a car. He told the clerk he'd been left behind by some fishing friends who'd gone off with some ladies they met. The clerk laughed and sent a car, and after a brief trip to the office, he signed the contract and drove away in a small, dark, nondescript sedan. He took Rosalie, or Jane, to a small restaurant near the motel, where they sat on the wooden terrace overlooking the slow current of the inlet. The sky to the east was darkening, and the scattered handful of fishermen along the banks were fading out of sight.

"What are we doing?" Rosalie wanted to know.

"Any suggestions?"

"You could turn in the suitcase. Leave it somewhere and call the police." She paused. "So far, you haven't committed anything except escaping, true? So far?"

He exhaled.

"Do you know what you're delivering?"

He shook his head.

"Any other options?" he asked her.

She looked quietly at him.

"I have some friends in Arizona who could take us in. Why don't we go there? Maybe they'll solve the case and forget about you."

He looked around the deck. No one seemed to be watching them.

"Do you suppose they have sent our descriptions everywhere? You are especially easy to spot with that hair."

"I can change it."

"You can go back to Connecticut, too. Why don't you, while you've done nothing?"

"No." She shook her head. "No, I'm staying."

"Why?"

"I want to." She looked into his eyes. "Don't you want me to?"

"I don't know where this is heading. Maybe a lot of trouble for you."

"I'll risk it." He studied her.

"Okay, but don't say I didn't give you the chance. And don't change your hair, okay? I like it."

"I won't. Either of those. So it's Arizona?"

He looked away from her.

"I want to go see my son."

"That's the first place they'll look for you."

"Maybe. I'll be careful. Wait for me."

They finished their meal without saying much else, and he left her at the room and headed down US 1, along thirty miles of shops and restaurants alternating with glittering motels and condominiums, each place in the sun lit by spotlights so it swept against the seaside sky like a grand mansion, each inhabited by hundreds of people instead of one family, each probably still believing it owned the earth and the sky.

Rosalie walked into their room and sat on the bed, listening to the car drive away alone, without Reed beside her for the first time since their escape, since they had met. Unable to sit still, she got to her feet and paced the room, kicking the boat shoes into the corner. She unbuttoned and removed the cotton shirt she had worn all day, unbuckled and peeled off the jeans she had walked ashore in. She bent forward at the waist, threading her fingers through her long hair, shaking it free, stood up, and smoothed the short cotton tee shirt she had worn underneath.

The room was drafty, and the floor bare, and she began pacing around briskly, pumping her arms until she arrived at the closet. She opened the door and looked inside, and the suitcase stared back at her like a ticking bomb. But the rest of the closet was bare, except for a gray raincoat on a hanger and a spare blanket wedged into a corner. She picked up the blanket and put it over her shoulders, reached in, and grabbed the handle of the suitcase. The bag wasn't too heavy, and with a little effort, she was able to lift it out into the room and to the middle of the floor. Then she sat down on the bed again and watched it as if it were alive. She tried to imagine Reed finding the name in the telephone book, showing up unannounced on a dirt road between two four-lane highways, parking under a palm tree, and crossing the lawn, made of bristly green grass hard as rubber, the small white house quiet except for a television set. She closed her eyes and listened to the waves outside, crashing steadily against the rocks behind the motel.

When she opened her eyes, the suitcase was still there.

Chapter 5

LINDA TERRAZZO SCANLON ANSWERED THE DOOR AND GASPED. "It's you," she said, blinking. It seemed minutes went by before she said to come in.

"I thought you were in Connecticut. At least my husband said you were. Are you this Fool?"

"Not anymore."

"Did you kill that man?"

"No."

"And they let you go?"

He looked around. They were alone.

"Has anyone contacted you? It's been days."

"No. Not a word from Bill since he called a week ago. He was my husband. But he left a couple of years ago."

She looked about to cry.

"God, how you've messed up my life. It isn't fair. I ought to hate you so much, but now I can't even do that. For years I hated you, and now you're here, and I can't even hate you like I wish I could."

"Linda, he told me you have a son. Our son."

"You can't see him." Her eyes widened.

"Why not?"

"What right do you have to? Where have you ever been when he needed you? To think I tried to kill myself over you, and you could only tell my girlfriends to take care of me. What kind of father have you ever been?"

"Linda, no one ever told me."

She lit a cigarette, her hands noticeably shaking.

"I was pregnant. That's why I told you I wanted to get married. You never even asked why. You just waited a week and then said we were through. You who I loved." She sagged down on the nearby couch; she had waited for so long to tell him off, and now here he was, and she had no more to say.

"Linda, I'm sorry. I truly am. We wouldn't have been happy. I couldn't have supported you. But you're right: I wronged you in a way I never knew. And I can't stay now. Please, can we bury what's past? I want to see our son, just meet him, and I'll never bother you again. All right?"

Linda began crying again. "He's not all right," she said.

"Why not?"

"He's dying. He has a rare form of leukemia. In fact, he's got very little time left. It's just as well; he had nothing to look forward to—no father, no future, just more scraping by every day."

He waited, and she slapped her hands together softly.

"You want to see him anyway? It isn't a pretty sight."

"Yes."

And so in a dark room, lit only by the moon through the trees outside the window, he saw the boy they had made years ago in a narrow college bed, balding and pale from the hospital radiation treatments, one eye swollen, his pencil-thin legs sticking out from under the sheet.

"Mommy?" a faint voice called.

"Yes, honey," his mother answered.

"Could I have some Sugar Joes?"

"Yes, okay." She looked at Reed and left the room.

"Who are you?" the voice asked.

"A friend of your mother's," he answered softly.

"That's good," the boy nodded. "She needs a friend."

He couldn't stand there any longer without crying. He went out to the kitchen and sat down. Linda ignored him until he began asking questions. When did he come home? Why wasn't he in the hospital? Why didn't she feed him something healthy, something with no sugar?

"The doctors say they can't do anything more for him, and he's always eaten that, and anyway, with so little time left, I'm not going to deny him anything he wants."

"What if he doesn't have to die?"

"What are you, a miracle worker? The best doctors in Florida say they can't help him."

He sat at the table and stared down the hall.

"Linda, doctors treat symptoms. Somewhere there's a secret to it. Will you let me help?"

"How?"

"I'll come back tomorrow and tell you. Right now, I have to go. Please let me help. And please don't tell anyone I was here. My life could depend on it."

She stood facing him; she started to sway as if she would fall into his arms, just like years ago, but she blinked and stopped herself.

"Please go," she said.

The frail voice sounded in the next room.

"Mommy," it said.

Linda Terrazzo Scanlon wiped the wet spots under her nose and started toward the back room, unable to understand both her amazement and her blankness that Rett Haskins had just been standing there. For years, she had hated the man, until her hatred turned to a distant contempt. Yet she had never wavered in her love for the boy he had fathered. And Timmy had returned her love in too many ways to count, his intelligence and sweetness undiminished by his disease. And then this afternoon he had asked if he was dying, and she had told him the truth, and Timmy had asked her—her son had asked her—to let it happen and not to be sad because he was ready. And she had cried until long after dark, until she had decided to do as he asked, to make them suffer no more, and to end the horrible treatments he'd been given of radiations, chemotherapy drugs, and blood transfusions, a treatment that had paralyzed his eye half open and half shut and made his entire body ache with a pain that never eased. And when she had made that decision, she had cried again until his father had appeared at her door as if from thin air.

As she entered his room, the moonlight had moved behind a tree, and it was dark.

"Mommy, will you stay here with me?"

"For a while, honey."

"Mommy."

"Yes."

"Please don't cry, okay?" Linda Scanlon sat on the carpet next to his bed for what she knew would be a long night. The sound of crickets across the canal seeped in the window as Timmy closed his left eye.

Chapter 6

—◦◦◦—

DYLAN REED KNOCKED TWICE AND SAID, "IT'S ME." THE LOCK opened, and he went in. She was wearing nothing but a thin tee-shirt, panties, and a raincoat. And as he reached the center of the room, she eagerly pressed herself against him. He put his hands under the raincoat and held onto her.

"Did you see him?"

"Yes." He sat down, and she waited.

"He's dying. He has leukemia."

She sat down on the bed next to him.

"He has a few days left."

"Oh, I'm so sorry," she answered helplessly. She put her face next to his and held him while he cried. When he stopped, she kissed his wet eyes, then stood up and dried his eyes with her tee-shirt.

"Come on," she said. She took his hand and led him right out the door. They began walking away from the cottages, along a walkway toward the ocean. Neither spoke until they reached the edge of a sandy, deserted beach; the waves were small and almost soundless at low tide, and the moon, slipping into the trees to the west, left the stars over the ocean at their brightest.

"Look over there." She pointed.

"What?"

"That's Orion. Four stars in a trapezoid, two each for shoulders and feet. In his upraised arm is the club of the warrior, and the three stars across his belt hold the sword. Each night he crosses the entire sky like a guardian, and it has been said he is the true guardian of this planet during its hours of darkness. I give him to you. Let him be your guiding spirit."

"Rosalie, this is no time to be cosmic."

"I'm not kidding. Listen to me. Geller taught you many powers. You can use them."

He turned and faced her. She was so beautiful it took his breath away. And the mention of Geller brought a wave he had let slip into the back of his mind--ideas, thoughts, residing in a whisper behind a curtain.

"How do you know about Geller?"

"I was his student, as were you. He asked me to look after you; he was afraid you were learning so fast, you would be unprepared."

"Unprepared for what?"

"There's a reality beyond this physical world. You and I are learning to walk in its light."

"Are you saying you're here because of Geller?"

"He sent me. I stayed on my own."

She reached in the pocket of her coat and drew out two small gray objects shaped like round buttons, the color of dry wood.

"Eat this," she said.

"What is it?"

"A mushroom. It will help you see. Chew it slowly."

He took one and popped it in his mouth, chewing it absentmindedly. It tasted old at first but felt good in his mouth.

"Tell me more about Orion," he finally asked.

"The belt is the center of the warrior, or more accurately, the stomach is the seat of his strength. The constellations of the zodiac, those are reference points of the sun and important for that reason, but Orion patrols the sky."

"Like Superman?" he asked, laughing, a laugh that itself came from his stomach, a laugh he could not control.

"Yes, like Superman, flying through the night looking for old ladies about to drive off cliffs." She laughed too, and he laughed harder, tears welling up in his eyes. And he was overwhelmed by the laughter and the sadness, split in half between the moment and the imminent tragedy he felt tied to, too late to change; he laughed, and tears flooded his eyes.

He lay back and stared at the stars. It was very late, and shooting stars were frequent, almost one a minute, it seemed, although he had no idea how slowly the time was passing. Orion had a bright blue star and a bright red one; he remembered staring at it long ago, as a child in Connecticut, when it shone above his bedroom window. He had always felt safe under it, but had never known why that was.

Rosalie leaned over him.

"Rett, there's one more thing."

"Just one?"

"Yes," she replied with her own soft, musical laugh.

"I'm here on my own. I'm here because I love you."

He reached around her waist, drew her to him, and kissed her. He lay back as she wriggled herself into a comfortable position on top of him, spreading the coat open, opening his belt and zipper, pressing herself against his skin, until he had found his way inside her. Her skin felt so alive, so smooth and luminous, and he floated on a wave of her shuddering, as with each rise and fall she called him with her breathing.

Covered only by the trench coat and Rosalie, who lay sleepily across half his body, he watched the stars. As if speaking to himself, he knew Rosalie would be with him from now on, and in the light of the mushroom, he knew he would not be going home to Chicago, to his apartment, to Lena, or to his short stories, ever again. But he was not sad; he was letting go, letting go of his entire life, taking events one at a time.

She stirred.

"Jane," he said.

"No," she murmured, "I'm Rosalie."

"I'm Dylan Reed now from now on. It's the only way. Call me that."

"I'm Rosalie," she repeated. "And you are Dylan Reed, no doubt about it. It sounds exciting. Is it?"

He turned her over and crawled between her legs. She shivered eagerly, and they moved together until their breathing turned into an audible chorus of "oh yes, oh yes," their limbs and muscles stretching in every direction until they collapsed together beneath the stars.

The lovers lay asleep on the beach. Orion made his nightly rounds like a deaf-mute town crier, smoothly protecting the skies as he had done for millions of years, and would do for millions more while earth cooled, peopled, and disappeared from existence in a piece of time too small for him to notice with more than a trace of sadness.

In a dream, Reed was a thousand miles away, in a jail cell, where he kissed a beautiful stranger. A voice said, "You cannot," and he rose into the sky, where it was still a blue day; they joined in an embrace, and when they separated, he fell into the sea to a depth he could not have endured were he awake. And when he came up he flew into the air, alternating the fallings and the flyings beneath the slowly changing sky.

The last descent left him standing on the beach, naked. He knew Rosalie was there and called to her, only to hear his voice as the voice of a child, and the words to say, "I need him. I need him." In the distance, he saw a grown man, standing at the water's edge; in the dream's knowledge, he knew he was the father of himself, the son, and yet the father was Timmy, his son, and he was Reed, the father, watching as a child. And there was Rosalie, helpless, as the figure of Timmy walked unyielding into the sea, leaving the child to his endless flying and falling into the sea.

In the dream, he grew older and returned to the jail cell, where he kissed a beautiful stranger. A voice said, "You cannot," and the dream froze. Reed dreamed and that he awoke and walked away; had he turned, he would have seen Rosalie and himself, lying curled in her raincoat, but he did not have time. He walked down the sand to a table that was set out upon it. There were three chairs, and only two were occupied, so he settled down in the third. He looked up and saw Lina across from him, although she did not look up. To his right sat Linda, dealing cards to the three of them. Each of them turned over a card, betting seashells in silence. They were a king and queen.

"I see," said Linda. She put a card in the middle, face down. Lina tossed another seashell into the pile.

"I'll look," she said. She turned it over.

It was the lovers, entwined in their nakedness.

All three stared at the card. Lina spoke first.

"It's yours, Reed." She called him his new name.

He picked up the card and stood up. He kissed Lina, with love but without desire. Then he kissed Linda in the same manner. Each returned his kiss with the same affection and naturalness, and he began walking down the beach again.

He came to a large shell. He put his ear against it, hoping to hear the sea; but he heard a strange din of human conversation, until a voice began to emerge from the noise. It was the voice he knew from the jail cell, the man who had told him his wife's address, the man who had sent him to Timmy.

"Please, speak my name," it moaned. "Please, speak my name. Have pity on me, please. We have loved a woman. We have known a son, and now I am your prisoner."

"Don't trust this man," a second voice cut in. It was Major Gilley's voice, and it startled Reed; he almost woke up, and he felt himself slipping back to his sleeping form, his wave on its ebb.

"I repeat, do not trust this man," the major intoned. "He's out to hunt you down. To the south is the sea." And the voice, repeating itself, sank beneath the threshold of volume.

Reed walked slowly back, asking himself how much longer he could hold the policeman a prisoner. He studied the card in his hand until he heard the voice say, "You cannot." He turned around, and Geller was standing a few feet away, Orion's bright red star shining through the transparency of his hair.

Reed held up the card.

"I can," he answered. Geller smiled slightly, turned and walked away.

Reed picked Roslie up in his arms. He kissed her hair softly as he carried her back to their cabin.

He awoke in the morning and spoke before he was fully cognizant, in that instant of suspended consciousness between one's sleeping and waking selves.

"Scanlon," he said.

The chase was on.

Chapter 7

——◦/◦/◦——

Iᴛ ᴡᴀꜱ 2:00 ᴘ.ᴍ., Fʀɪᴅᴀʏ. Rᴇᴇᴅ ᴡᴀʟᴋᴇᴅ ᴛᴏ ᴛʜᴇ ᴘʜᴏɴᴇ ʙᴏᴏᴛʜ ᴏɴ the tree and called Anthony Frascone.

"This is Reed."

The voice immediately started talking.

"Go to the drug store in the mall near you on the highway. See the blond-haired boy at the counter. Got that?"

"Wait. Hold on. There's one more condition to this."

There was silence on the other end. He waited a few seconds and continued.

"I need your help. It's not money or cops."

Ten seconds went by.

"What is it?"

"I have a friend whose young son is ill and needs help. He can't get it here. If you are what I think you are, you are rich and have connections. You wouldn't let your own son down on this."

"So?"

"He has leukemia. Where are the rich people sending their kids these days?"

"I see," said the voice. "You know, they aren't doing much better with it than anyone else."

"What can you arrange? This is a boy's life we're talking about."

"Should I remind you, you have a job to do and you're a perfect stranger to me?"

"The job will be done if you'll help."

There was more silence, so he continued.

"I know there must be places where people like you would go your-self. And it's not too expensive compared to what we're dealing with here, is it? It's done on connections, and I need yours."

He had run out of words. The operator cut in to ask for another fifty cents. He put in the coins and waited. Two minutes later, the operator cut in again.

"Will that be all?" she asked.

He hung up and grabbed Rosalie from their cabin. He took the suit-case out of the closet and stared at it. There it was, the grease for all these wheels and all this disease. Well, he told himself, it's either got to pay for something worthwhile or he would bury it where it will be worthless forever. He threw it in the trunk, pushed her into the car, and started up.

She was complaining louder and louder the whole time, until her voice reached a yell.

"What's the rush?"

He drove the car around the dirt road behind the cabins, about a hundred feet from the motel, and turned it off. No more than a minute later, a black sedan pulled into the motel yard. A man in sunglasses and a suit entered the office, emerged a second later, and walked straight to their cabin.

"Watch," Reed said.

The man kicked open the cabin door, drawing out a revolver as he disappeared inside. He came back out and went to the phone. He made a call, got back in his car, and drove away.

Reed started the car and followed him out to the highway. They turned left and went three miles before entering a large mall, heading toward a pharmacy in the far corner. He parked and left the door un-locked and went inside. Reed got there in time to see the man take an envelope from the blond cashier and turn around.

The man came back to the car and got in and sat down. Reed sat up quickly in the back, reached both arms over the seat, and grabbed the man's armpits. He yanked him over the top of the seat, reached under his left arm, and took the revolver from its holster, exactly where he had seen the man place it minutes before. Then he slid out from under him in a motion so smooth that, when the man landed on the back seat, he looked straight ahead into his own gun.

"Get out. Slowly. We're going to a telephone, and if no one is stupid, no one will be hurt."

They went to a corner, where the phones were secluded by potted palms all around. In the heat of a Florida September, it was the three o'clock time of day when nothing was moving.

"Call Frascone," he told the man.

The man dialed the number and handed him the phone. He pushed it back.

"Say hello."

The man looked at him and said, "It's me."

Reed grabbed the phone.

"And this is me. Now listen. Your man here failed. I don't want to have to give him and his suitcase to the cops. I'd rather complete this deal, but I want help for this kid. Do I get it from you or someone else?"

"Wait, wait," Frascone said. "I called someone. Please excuse my … precautions. All right. All right. There is a place in Jamaica. They use papaya enzymes, I'm told. There's a 3:00 a.m. flight, and the doctor—his name is Renardo—will meet you. You'll have to get your own ticket."

"Where's the flight?"

"Miami International."

"Is this on the level?"

"Yes. You can believe me."

"All right. All right, as you say." He waved the barely hidden gun at the other man.

"Is that envelope what I'm supposed to do?"

The man, wide-eyed, nodded.

"All right, I have my instructions, then. See you." He started to hang up when he heard the voice speak on the phone.

"What?"

"Your boy," Frascone said. "I hope you save him."

They still had some cash left. Rosalie insisted they get some new clothes, and with the off-season prices, they could afford to change their appearances completely.

"Why bother getting these?" he asked when she picked a suit for him, a gray pinstripe model with wide lapels, something a man would wear to the office twice a week.

"The police are looking for you, aren't they? But they won't expect you to be walking around looking like a million bucks. They think you're a ... a—"

"A fool?" he interrupted. He got the idea.

At 6:15, he went to the bus station in West Palm Beach, a seedy-looking building that could have been in a small town in Mexico. He bought a ticket for Miami and went to the lockers. He put the suitcase into one, locked it, and went to the men's room.

Two stalls from the end, he put a dime in the slot, went in, and sat down. He noticed a pair of dark shoes to his right and immediately heard two knocks on the separation between them.

What if this is some old pervert? he thought, but he took a breath and tapped twice back. A hand slowly unfolded under the separator, palm up and backward, like an old screwball pitcher gets after turning his hand inside out for years and years.

He placed the key in the man's hand, stood up, and left the stall. Feeling a cool gust of a six-o'clock breeze, he turned toward an open window, yawning over a parking lot for the nearby pink hotel.

What do you know? he said to himself. So this is big-time crime. Might as well put the cherry on the sundae. He jumped onto the windowsill and down to the parking lot, laughing; it was all run like some crazy clockwork, on schedule and with all the parts meshing together.

∽

Five minutes later, the dark shoes walked into the lobby of the bus station with his locker key. Four armed officers and a plainclothes detective threw him against the wall, pressing a handgun against his back.

"Spread 'em," the detective spat out like somebody who's seen all the cop movies and has waited for this day for a long time. He was young and smart, younger than the four uniformed men who carried the artillery and did the physical stuff, so smart that he believed they were carrying out justice, doing something worthwhile with his intelligence and education. But he wasn't smart enough to realize that he too was in a uniform, filling a slot, and later that year, his superiors would take him off the case, not because he couldn't solve it but because he might. For now, though, his next major move was critical for his reputation, and he knew the spotlight was on him as he thought.

"All right," he said, "where's the other guy?"

Chapter 8

———◀◉◉◉▶———

THEY SAT QUIETLY IN THE CORNER OF A SMALL RESTAURANT ON Route 1. It was one of those places built before the 1960s real estate boom and was a bit seedy. On the other hand, they were alone, and that was a safe feeling.

"Reed, I'm sorry I was so difficult this morning," she said. "I didn't know we were in danger."

"It's okay, really."

"Look, it isn't okay. We've got some talking to do," she said, letting her voice soften. "At least there's something I've got to say."

"Say it, then."

She took a deep breath.

"We're not in a position to get careless. First of all, you for sure and probably me by now are both wanted criminals. Anyone might recognize us."

"Even here?"

"Are you kidding? Every place in America and who knows where else has heard of the Fool and knows you've escaped."

"Wait a minute. Do they know that? What if the police keep that to themselves?"

She paused.

"Good question. Well, by now, Scanlon's on your trail, and since you're following the trail he set for you, he knows where you're going. Do you?"

"Jamaica, tonight."

"They'll be waiting for you."

"I'll be careful."

He studied her.

"Is this some kind of goodbye speech?" he asked.

"No, no, that's not it." She shook her head and looked around the quiet restaurant. "I don't know. We may not always be together."

She looked up, their eyes met, and they both smiled.

"Who knows, maybe we might."

They sat there silently a minute before he reached across and touched her face.

"Rosalie," he said softly, "Geller told you to look after me, didn't he?"

"Yes."

"Didn't it ever occur to you he meant for me to look after you, too?"

She smiled again.

"Then what am I supposed to do when you go to Jamaica?"

"I don't know. What do you want to do?"

"I'd like to wait for you," she said.

"You know, you can still say you were kidnapped and walk away from this."

"I know."

He looked around the nearly empty restaurant.

"Or you can drive," he said, "to Arizona."

"Well," she said reluctantly. Then her tone shifted, softened. "Do you really think this is the best thing?"

"What you mean?"

"That suitcase was full of drugs, stuff that's going to kill a few people. That's what's paying for Timmy's life, isn't it?"

He thought a moment.

"I didn't open it," he said. "I don't know what's inside. Probably no excuse, but it's true. But we're riding this wave now, and if it's right, it will work out."

"Riding this wave?" she mused. "What a way to put it."

cSD

It was 11:00 p.m. when Reed stepped through the shadows along the fringe of Linda Scanlon's dirt road. He guessed whatever danger he might be in would expect his arrival by car, and he noticed two cars with men in them, each sitting about a hundred feet from the house in each direction.

He came to the back window and looked into the dark room for a long time before his eyes adjusted. Timmy was lying on the bed. The room was empty, his mother in the front of the house.

He took out the pocket knife he'd bought and quietly cut a hole in the window screen, then reached inside and released the catch. The screen slid away, and he looked once around to see if he was alone. He was. He picked up the cinder block he'd found on the patio, moved it beneath the window, and balanced on it. He got his head and shoulders in. Timmy made no sound; he got his whole body in and landed softly on the thick carpet.

He went to the bed and put his hand over Timmy's mouth as he reached underneath him to lift him up, but he stopped.

Timmy was stone cold.

The door opened, and Linda stood there; she couldn't even be shocked anymore, she said. She was too drained.

"So, it's you again."

"Linda."

"He's been dead for an hour, Rett. They're on their way now. And you were going to take him away from me."

"I was going to take him to a doctor who might've helped, Linda. That's all. I'm sorry."

"You're always sorry, Rett. He's beyond your help now." She began to walk toward him. "You know, he slipped into a coma two nights ago, just a few hours after you left. But he asked me who you were, so I told him. You know what he said?"

"What?"

"He said it was nice to meet you. Nice to meet you. Oh, Rett, he was so special, so sweet. Why is life so cruel to people like Timmy?"

He couldn't answer.

She was getting more depressed, but Reed couldn't help noticing she was worn out and seemed to have no tears left.

"Maybe it's better this way," she said, half to herself. Then she turned toward Timmy and whispered, "Bye, honey," so delicately, he thought his heart would break. She turned toward him now.

"And you, where were you going to take him?"

"Jamaica."

"And now?"

But he just looked at her and knew she couldn't know. He couldn't tell her, and she didn't really want him to. And she drew herself up to him, and to his surprise, she put her arms around him and her face on his shoulder, and he remembered holding this woman twelve years ago.

"Rett," she whispered. "Thank you for Timmy." She looked into his eyes, and they both began to cry and fight it.

He spoke to her firmly now, but softly, and with more love than he ever knew he had for her.

"Linda," he said, "start over now. We loved each other, and now you should love someone else. Timmy would want that, too—for you not to be lonely. Move away from here if you have to, but pull your life together."

"And what about you?"

"Forget me. Just ... forget me. Think of me sometimes if you want to, but start again." He wished he could say something that would help, that could make her see a way forward, but he had no words. He reached into his pocket, drew out the last of his thousand dollars, and gave her two hundred of the four hundred he had left. Maybe he still had a few days' credit on the card.

He wanted to be allowed the time to grieve, but he had no time, and it would have to wait. He recalled seeing him walk into the sea two nights earlier and knew he had dreamed Timmy's lapse into the coma.

"Goodbye, Linda," he told her. He wanted to say more, but there was nothing to say now, and he was already climbing out the window when she answered.

"Goodbye, Rett."

He was across the back lots and in the trees when the ambulance arrived and two attendants plus a plainclothes detective and FBI agent Bill Scanlon entered the small house seconds later.

"He was here, Bill," Linda said.

"WHAT?"

"And he's gone."

"Tell me where, Linda. Tell me now. This isn't just our problem. You are an accessory now if you don't tell me."

"All right, Bill, I'll tell you. He was going to Jamaica."

In a short time, Timmy's body was riding through the Palm Beach night, a soft breeze was blowing through the palm leaves, and Linda Terrazzo Scanlon sat by the window of the car, staring out, steeling herself for the ordeal of burial that was to come. Silently, she mouthed the words, as if she were speaking to her son: "Wherever you are going, please let it be better than the hell you've been through."

⌒∽⌒

The plainclothes detective with Scanlon knew the route.

"Jamaica," he said. "That's the 3:00 a.m. flight. Wait a minute. Could he have been the drop man we picked up on that tap this afternoon?"

At Miami International Airport, passengers to Jamaica that night would be delayed without explanation for several minutes, and an FBI agent and a detective would lose another night's sleep awaiting the arrival of the man wanted separately by each of them. A doctor in Jamaica would waste the night expecting a patient who would never arrive. And although Scanlon would, through a one-way glass partition, peer carefully into each face, expecting any kind of disguise, he would not find the one who was becoming an obsession for him. Somewhere inside, he knew he was afraid of the man he wanted to catch—not afraid of being shot or injured but of being confronted with something beyond the narrow confines of the regulations and laws he was sworn to. He wanted to face the man once alone, but in a safe situation with no escape, and get to the bottom of what he remembered from the jail cell. It was a cause for anger, because he could not explain it, even to himself.

By 4:00 a.m., Scanlon put out the word for highway roadblocks on every interstate and main highway, but he didn't expect much to turn up. Meanwhile, on the turnpike north, Reed tried to sort things out. Linda would probably say he'd been there so the police wouldn't continue camping in her street; and soon, they should expect the highway patrol to be looking closely at every redheaded woman or blond male driver.

The sky was getting light in the east as they passed Orlando and its mile after mile of tourist attractions blooming in the Florida swamps. They were heading north and west as he turned on the radio, scanning the dial at low volume so Rosalie would not awaken. He tried several stations before abandoning the radio to some generic rock song, and when that ended, the news came on.

"Murder in Fort Lauderdale," a woman's voice sounded urgently. "Financier Anthony Frascone was found dead late last night in a small restaurant. The millionaire money man was shot, police say, by an unidentified gunman while eating dinner. Police spokesmen say an investigation is already underway. More after this."

Rosalie woke up and heard the last part of it.

"I guess that wave ran its course all the way," she said.

Chapter 9

———⟆⟆⟆———

"**R**OSALIE, TELL ME SOMETHING. I FELT A SURGE OF ... CLARITY when I knew Timmy was dead, as if he gave me something. Is that possible?"

"Maybe you should meditate on it. You may find something there."

"Well, while you were asleep I saw a roadblock ahead. In my mind. Somewhere near Gainesville, in a place we can't turn around. So I want you to do exactly as I say."

"All right."

"I'm going to get off at this exit and get in the trunk."

"But Reed, they're still going to recognize me."

"Not if you do what I say. This is a busy exit, and it's almost morning. Pick up a hitchhiker, a safe-looking one. Then tease him. Act like you're trying to seduce him. Tell him you want him to stay with you at your house in Georgia or something. Anything so he'll say you're together; they won't be looking for you with a different man."

"You're crazy."

"Do it. It'll work." He pulled the car into a parking lot full of trucks, stopped it, and started to get out.

"You're getting in the trunk? You'll be listening the whole time."

"That's right," he grinned at her. "Pretend I'm not there. I'll be busy anyway."

"Doing what?"

"Think of me as someone, someone contemplating a light of his own." He laughed, but she didn't get the joke. He climbed in the trunk and pulled it shut. It was clean and empty, like a car rental. They had taken the time to renew it for three weeks and would have to leave it before long. First, he wanted to get out of the state.

Rosalie had her choice of not one but three hitchhikers, so she sat by the road and looked them over. The middle one on the ramp looked like a college kid, with shaggy brown hair and a brown sport jacket. She decided he looked less risky than the others and nothing like Reed. She took a deep breath and unbuttoned the top two buttons on her blouse and the bottom two buttons from the six on her skirt, hiking it up so her legs were subtly displayed several inches above her knees. She looked in the mirror, found her eyes a little rough around the edges, and started thinking up a story.

She pulled the car up to the college man, and he got in, and as his eyes widened, she knew he was impressed. Once on the highway, she started to talk.

"My name is Jane. What's yours?" It was Allen. She asked him about himself and it took three or four minutes before he started to relax. She wished she knew where Gainesville was and how much time she had.

"You know, you're kind of cute," she said. He turned toward her. "Look, um, I just left my old man. I mean, he had another girlfriend for months anyway, and that's why my eyes look like this." She waited for him to say something.

Finally, he spoke.

"He was cheating on you?"

She knew she had him.

"Hey, you're nice. I'm feeling kind of bad right now. Maybe you could sit a bit closer to me?" She reached out her hand, and he took it and slid over. She could tell he was getting excited and knew he might try to touch her at any time.

Reed, meanwhile, was somewhere else, having a private conversation with the idea of Geller.

"Am I on a negative cycle with all this dealing and people dying?" he asked.

"That depends," a voice answered somewhere. He drifted onto a plane where he was no longer conducting a dialogue, just listening. It faded in and out, but it helped him to envision a grassy field waving in the wind; it fixed his concentration.

"You were never part of the drug cycle," the voice inside continued. "You are an outsider all the way."

"Then who killed that guy in Connecticut?"

"He's died many times, none of them by your hand. Both the major and the murdered agent had their own reasons for being killed."

It didn't make any sense, and he wondered how he could ask himself anymore. Did he really fight in the French and Indian War? But no matter what specifics he wanted to know, the voice inside continued with its own agenda.

"All things are true. These are merely descriptive things you remember better than others. Remember, all things are also false, forms you must leave behind at some future time. Your course will make itself clear in its own way. It's up to you to be strong. I can tell you, you will have to lead others and also act on your own intuition more than you've ever done, but such responsibility goes with the gifts you're developing. And you will need another teacher soon, one who will take you where I cannot."

"Who's that?"

"You will know when the time is ready." Reed was beginning to drift away from the dialogue; the grass field was fading. He knew he should wonder how he could really be talking with Geller, but he simply suspended his usual judgment to believe what he heard.

"And Rosalie?"

"Rosalie is a strong and intelligent woman, more intelligent than you are sometimes. You are very fortunate she's also a good actress."

Up front, Rosalie was both dreading the roadblock and hoping it would happen soon, for Allen had his hand on her leg and was sweating a bit. She decided to push it a little.

"Look, Allen, when we get a couple of hours up the road, I know a nice place we can stop and spend a little time together. Would you like that?"

"Why don't we pull off the road now?"

"No, honey, it'll be worth the wait. I promise." She reached over and put her hand on his slacks and squeezed his leg.

"You'll see," she said. She felt stupid, but it was working.

"Oh, all right. I can wait a few miles," he said petulantly. But he wasn't letting up; he started kissing her around the throat and made her squirm, but she couldn't risk turning him off, so she let him. He was just trying to get under her shirt when the car rounded a bend and the roadblock was dead ahead.

"Stay here, honey. It's just some silly thing," she told him. He moved his hands off her, and she breathed a little easier.

She handed the officer the driver's license they had given her on the boat. She hadn't used it but had memorized the details and wondered if it would pass a check. She decided not to risk it.

She bent forward and saw the officer's eyes zero in on her open blouse. He took the license to phone it in, but he didn't move, trying to make conversation and keep staring at her.

She opened the door of the car and got out, and as he studied the license of Jane Delours, Florida resident, she kicked off a shoe and stroked his leg with her foot. The officer looked at her, and she stood facing him on the far side of the other policeman, stopping traffic. His hand hung loosely at his side, and she slid against it so it touched her hip, and he understood as she pressed herself against him. She unzipped his trousers and reached in.

"Be careful," she whispered. "Don't let them see us."

She kept it up until he hissed softly and leaned onto her for a moment, and he didn't call in her license. He tried to get his hand under her skirt, but she pushed him away and started to get back in her car.

"I have to go now," she told the officer. "You had your fun."

Outmaneuvered, he started to ask the hitchhiker for his identification.

"I don't have any," the kid said. She hadn't counted on that.

"Look, you got what you wanted. You know you'd better just let us go."

The cop stood there, working it out. He looked across toward the other officers, working other lanes; one of them was staring at him.

"All right," he said, a bit dazed. "You're not who we wanted anyway. But get yourself some ID."

She drove in silence to the next exit. The boy tried to get his hands on her again, but she pushed him away. She drove the car off the highway to a restaurant parking lot and pulled in, then turned off the engine.

"You'd better get out."

"What about this place we're going to?"

"Just GET OUT!" she shouted with fury, and when he didn't move, she got out quickly, went around back, and opened the trunk.

Reed appeared at the passenger door and yanked it open, grabbing the boy by the shoulders and pulling him out; the boy tried to swing at him but missed. Reed got in and slammed the door, and in a moment, they were on the highway again.

Neither of them said a word for miles, until Rosalie looked at him and took a deep breath.

She exhaled.

"You'd better treat me real nice today."

Chapter 10

———⟨ᴓ/ᴓ/ᴓ⟩———

IT WAS MANY UNEVENTFUL HOURS BEFORE THEY SPOKE TO EACH OTHER again with any tenderness; she drove in silence and he did not press her to converse. They picked up an all-night country station from New Orleans and left it on in the background, giving out the weather in the entire eastern half of the country, from Michigan to Florida and back to the great river, now one hundred miles ahead on the interstate. Then, when it was late, and the stars were pinpoint clear, Reed heard her clear her throat.

"We've got some talking to do."

"I'm listening."

"Have you made any sense of everything that's happened?" she asked, like a schoolteacher expecting a correct answer.

"You mean, do I have any plans?" he countered. "Not really."

"Perhaps you're thinking too literally, too much on the horizontal."

"What's that supposed to mean?"

"Maybe you're concentrating too hard on the mechanics of all this. Do you think your role here is just to keep escaping from being tried for these things you haven't done?"

"I'm a bit overwhelmed by it. It seems like a day or two ago, I was looking at the house where I was a kid. Since then, I've been in a two-hundred-year-old war, accused of killing somebody I never saw, sailed to Florida, committed a crime, lost a son, and now we're running," he finished, then laughed quietly.

"I guess I am feeling a little sorry for myself," he sighed. "It's a lot to sort out."

"Maybe you're not supposed to sort it out. You've forgotten a couple of things here. Look, Geller told me you were being lifted up onto a new plane. You're not an ordinary runaway, are you? I saw you stop the time when you kept that policeman from the gun in the cell. I know I didn't walk back from the beach the other night. I saw your entire dream, as if it were really happening, right there on the sand."

"I don't feel right talking about these things."

"Listen, I asked Gellar that. He said if something is unclear or troubling, ask away. He told me never to brag or make a mere demonstration of anything, but learning is what it's about."

She waited. He took a deep breath.

"You saw my dream?" She nodded.

"Then you know about Lina, and Linda too. And now I'm here with you."

"You told Geller you could."

"Well, I suppose I can." He looked over at her. "Look, I'd like to say I understand it all, but I don't."

She took her eyes off the road for a long moment to look into his.

"All that's happening has a purpose. I'd say that purpose was to transform you into a different sort of person, and it could only be done this way, by pulling the rug out from under you. So now you have no home you can safely go to, and if you stand still long enough, the police will catch you—or us, I should say. On the other hand, it's for the better, isn't it? What did you have that made you alive? Now you're fighting for your very existence, and with something you never dreamed was within you. You're alive, baby. You are alive, and you've been given a hand to play out, if I read your dream correctly."

He sat, silently listening to her.

"Look," she continued, "your whole destiny has just opened up to you. From this moment on you are free to go anywhere, do anything that you can back up. You're on a ledge, and you can either keep staring over the side or accept it and act out your part. Geller told me to tell you this."

"All right."

"But I want to add something."

He waited. They passed an exit sign.

"I know you loved Lina, and here you are with me. I'm going to take us to my friends in the Southwest. Then I will go wherever you send me or stay with you, whichever you wish. I believe I'm meant to love you, and Geller told me to take care of you, but you'll be on your own. I will only stay with you if you want me to."

He sat and watched her. Then he moved across the seat and held her in his arms, remaining there until they reached an exit, and she turned off and pulled into a gas station.

"We need gas," she said. "And food." She took out a small handbag from under the seat, found a baseball cap and pushed her hair under it, put on dark glasses, grabbed some cash from the purse, and got out.

The station was on a two-lane road in the country; across the pavement, a phone booth stood in front of a rundown shack with no sign. He got out and stood by the car, and she came around to his side and leaned against him.

"I'm going to call my place in Chicago," he said. "See what happens." He stood there, hands on his hips. "And from now on, I'm Dylan Reed. I have no past, then, a fresh start. You sure you want this?"

She put her arms around his neck and kissed him.

Across the highway, he dialed the long-ago Chicago phone number, trying the credit card; it was refused. He fumbled through his pockets and found some coins, enough that in seconds, it was ringing, and his heart was pounding. But the voice that answered was a man's voice, and it sounded like it belonged. Had they already moved him out?

"Is Lina there?"

"No. She won't be home until later."

"Then who's this?"

"This is Richard. Who's this?"

"Are you living there?" he asked, almost laughing.

"You got a lot of nerve," the voice answered. "Of course I do, so don't call again, creep." He hung up.

Inside, Rosalie surveyed the scant collection of chips, pretzels, and cigarettes, and asked if there were somewhere to eat in the area.

"This time a night, only place open is across the street," the man drawled.

Across the street was the dingy bar, frequented by county regulars who didn't mind the thick smoke and cheap liquor, for one good reason: it had a roulette wheel, around which a small crowd gathered noisily. Seated at the booth in the far corner, Reed told Rosalie about his phone call.

"She's already got someone else living with her, in my apartment. Imagine that?" He laughed.

"What's so funny?" she answered. "So do you."

He looked at her seriously for a moment, then laughed again.

Meanwhile, the long-distance operator had traced the credit card number back to a list and called the troopers.

"Information says this fellow Reed is in the area, just made a call."

"Reed? Who's that?"

"I don't know. Just a number on the screen to me."

"Okay, where then?"

"That old place out in the county, the Wheel of Fortune."

The desk man set up. That place, he said aloud, I told the chief sooner or later we're going to get caught for that place.

"Okay, I'll send a man," he said and hung up.

Five minutes later, the uniformed state trooper walked into the bar that paid for his daughter's private school. Officer Shifflett was tall and hard-bodied, and rumor had it he had killed that black man out on the highway last year. But he also knew faces, and when he saw two he'd noticed that morning, it was more than a phony credit card scam he was looking at. It was a promotion, a reward, and a game he had to play.

"Well, it means I can't feel guilty loving you," Reed said, trying to smooth talk her.

"Not so fast, buster." She squinted, jabbing his chest with her finger. "You still owe me for this morning. You had better be nice."

"That's right, buddy, you'd better be nice," a third voice leaned into the conversation.

"I beg your pardon?" Rosalie replied, looking straight into his face.

"Don't bother," the officer snorted back, sliding into the booth next to her, facing across from Reed.

"Now listen to me, you two. I know who you and this little lady are. Don't try to fake it. I know. I memorize faces. But I can't arrest you here, this spot doesn't exist. So I'm going to be a sporting man about it."

"How's that?" Reed spoke for the first time.

"It's thirty-seven miles to the Mississippi River. Get in your car and drive. If you make it before I catch y'all, it's my tough luck."

"And if you catch us?"

"Maybe I'll take this little lady here as my payment on the wager." He leered across at Reed. "What do you say? Unless you want to concede right now." He put his arm around Rosalie.

Reed squinted at him and caught his eyes, and to Officer Shifflett, it seemed as if the steel ball stopped rolling around and the paper money stopped being passed across the room.

"Listen to me, Officer. You will not get up until someone slaps you." He turned to Rosalie and grabbed her hand.

"Let's go."

They got back onto the highway. Thirty-seven miles. How long did they have? For the first time, Reed became aware the car he was driving, a new but not especially fast sedan. It had a good radio, air conditioning, tinted glass, and power seats, and it would not go faster than ninety. They had made about seven miles when Reed pulled off at the next exit, came to a stop at the end of the ramp, and turned left under the highway, off into a dark and unlit expanse of trees.

"What are you doing?" she asked finally.

"Getting off that highway," he replied.

"Well, in that case," she said, "let's look at a map." She unfolded the road atlas she had bought.

In the distance, the road was coming to a T. They came to a stop as she found the page.

"If we're where I think we are," she began, "take a right."

In the bar, the wheel spun twice more before the bartender spotted the trooper alone in the booth, his hat on the bench. He went over and spoke to him but got no response. He stared at him for a moment, then slapped his face. Shifflett awoke, and without speaking, he jumped up and was out the door, minutes behind, doing 120 miles an hour, gaining half a mile a minute. He passed the next exit and, crossing over the two-lane highway, had a long view in both directions. When he spied the taillights in the distance, he stopped abruptly, screeching to a halt on the shoulder; he backed up a hundred yards and looked across the open land to where a car stopped, sat a moment, and turned right.

On the lonesome stretch of highway, Reed looked into the rearview mirror and saw headlights in the distance, gaining fast. He tried to straddle both lanes, but after a mile, the trooper passed them, turned on his light, and slowed down, forcing them to the shoulder. The cop got out and drew his gun, and when he was halfway to their car, Reed stepped on the gas.

"Fuck!" the trooper yelled, and jumped out of the way. Their head start lasted about a quarter mile. But this time, the trooper pulled in behind them and matched his speed at seventy, sitting right on their tail.

"He doesn't know how to take us. He can't shoot because he wants you, and he can't take us by hand. We're going for it."

For fifteen miles, he tried to lock eyes in the mirror with the man behind them, but it was too dark, and the headlights blurred the exchange. Then they cleared the last hill, and way off in the distance, they saw the roadblock. There was no way to cross the river.

He let the car slow down, way down; still, the trooper would not pass, waiting just behind them, a few feet from their bumper. They slowed to a stop. The trooper sat in his car. He was giving Reed no second chance to hypnotize him.

It was a stalemate: 4:30 in the morning, no traffic, and no chance to get away, and they were sitting on the shoulder, on a small hilltop from where they could see the river. The wheel had ground to a stop.

"Reed," Rosalie said, "suppose I went back there, as if he won and—"

"No."

"I wouldn't let him touch me or anything."

"No."

It was beginning to get lighter behind them, when shapes seem ghostly in the morning mist. Reed found his mind strangely quiet for the circumstances, beginning to drift into the abstract. How, he wondered, did the policeman find us? He retraced the day up to when they had stopped. He'd made a phone call. With a credit card. The free ride was over. Yet he felt calm, quiet enough to feel a distant, low rumble in the earth, and as he idly let his eyes drift to look in the rearview mirror, a train entered the valley behind them with a long, low whistle. And it kept coming, with no end in sight; he jolted.

Rosalie, who had drifted off to her own thoughts, started as well. Instinctively, she turned to spot the train, but Reed was already starting the engine.

"What are you doing?" she asked.

"It's time," he said, "or our number is up." He pulled away quickly, the officer behind them doing the same. It was to be a dogfight. He looked in his mirror, slowly building up speed on the highway until he was doing fifty, halfway to the roadblock ahead, the policeman right off his bumper. At seventy-five, he was less than a quarter-mile from the trooper formation, blocking the bridge across the river like tanks making their last stand. Policemen brandishing rifles, squinting into the low light, were stationed behind the cars parked diagonally on the highway as the trooper came up on his left, his faster car quickly overtaking them, a big smile on his face.

Read yanked the wheel to the right so hard, Rosalie fell across the seat against his arm, and for a moment he lost control, then regained it as the car went over the shoulder. It careened across the grass and onto the mud road between the highway and the tracks. He looked up, and the trooper was slowly coming around, first on two wheels, then down the shoulder. To his left, another patrol car turned on its lights and, with a screech, started the pursuit.

Reed's car dipped hard as it hit a hole, and the right front wheel clanked on its housing, but it held, and they sped down the mud road at fifty-five as the caboose came in sight.

He had a three-or four-length lead as it went by, and he hit the tracks at forty-five; with a high bounce, the right tires cleared the rail, and they were bouncing down the track onto the old railroad bridge, high over the Mississippi River, two patrol cars hot on their trail. The river looked miles wide, and every railroad tie was one jolt away from flying over the side; the rear car lost control seconds onto the bridge as his left-front tire went over the edge. The driver hit the brakes standing up, and the car stopped still, dangling high above the Big Muddy, rocking in place like a hammock. The driver got out and walked back.

"One down," said Rosalie, watching her side mirror.

Officer Shifflett would not quit, and as they bounced across the river, a bullet whizzed by his window, shattering the side mirror. Reed sped up slightly, but the pace was too hard for steering, and he had to slow down. He slunk low on the seat to where he could barely see the track ahead; they still had a few hundred feet of bridge to go when, looking up into the mirror, past the police car, he saw a second train coming up behind them, sparks flying from its undercarriage as it tried to stop. But it had entered the bridge too fast and was closing on them; the first car was scooped over the side, long since empty.

"Rosalie, we have to jump."

"What?"

"Jump, dammit, jump."

He couldn't wait. He opened his door and grabbed her by the wrist and dragged her as he went out the side. She yelled as she fell out behind him. For a perfect moment, they hung in the air as Reed yelled "I love you" to her, still holding her wrist. He pulled them together as they hit the water, wrapped tightly in each other's arms. They didn't hit bottom and came up fast as the train slammed into the patrol car, sandwiched between their sedan and the locomotive. With the terrifying shriek of metal and death, the police car was crushed and hurled over the side, landing like a tin coffin fifty yards away, where it sat momentarily and began to sink.

"Can you make it to shore?" Reed asked her.

"I think so," she answered as the current drew them quickly away from the bridge.

He swam over to the hulk drifting toward downstream and looked around for some access to the inside. It was all underwater, but the space where a windshield had been was now only a foot wide. Two eyes looked out.

"They're up there," a thin voice said. "You won. I will pay the bet. Don't go ashore. They're waiting. To the south is the sea."

The car began to sink as the current drew Reed away.

To the south is the sea. He knew the words well.

Making it to an overhanging limb, he spied Rosalie on the beach upriver and searchlights on the far bank.

"Rosalie, get back in the water," he called.

She stared at him blankly an instant before turning around. When she saw the lights coming toward her, she stepped off the bank and soon was beside him again, drifting down the muddy water, hugging the shore, staying in the shadows where they were difficult to see. They made it around a bend before the sun hit the river and farther down reached a fallen tree, where they held on and walked onto the bank. They huddled together, shivering, letting the sun dry them, keeping out of sight.

Chapter 11

———◦∕◦∕◦———

HAD MAN NEVER EXISTED, THE MISSISSIPPI RIVER WOULD STILL BE dirty, transporting uncountable tons of silt, driftwood, and mud from its shores and tributaries into the morass of its Delta, expanding slowly into the Gulf of Mexico. Without it, the backbone of North America would be uncleansed, much as a man would be if he did not sweat or excrete. But with man, the river has taken on uncountable tons of excrement, chemical fertilizers from farms, and industrial pollution from hundreds of miles of abuse.

Their clothes stinking and exhausted with hunger and lack of sleep, Reed and Rosalie slept through the day, hidden in the nearshore underbrush. As the sky turned red and deeper blue, they knew they had to move.

"To the south is the sea," Reed said. "The last time I took that route, I ended up in jail." He thought a moment and added, "Where I met you."

"I think we should try to head west," she answered. "Before we come to a town. Let's drift south a bit, then cross some unsettled areas. We need to get to where they haven't heard of us. Or don't care."

"What about food?" he asked. "And water?"

"We'll have to find some and fast. It's been done before."

He gathered some thick pieces of wood and assembled a makeshift raft, which he tied with his shirt and some green twigs he found on the bank. Gingerly, they floated along the muddy shore once again, careful to avoid being seen.

⌘

The official police report would list them as missing and presumed dead. William Scanlon, who had followed their trail to state police headquarters in North Louisiana, was presuming nothing. Any man who could wipe out several days of my life with his eyes cannot be regarded so lightly, he thought. But in a nation where the police are always hunting someone, his superior had other priorities.

"Scanlon, get back here today," the man barked into the phone. "I've had enough of this. Get back here and write a written report on these people, and spare no details. Then take a day off and report for another assignment. That's final." The line went dead.

He looked at the board in the next office, carrying today's murders, burglaries, and administrative attempts to dole out justice, state-police style, and he found it completely uninteresting.

The desk man squinted at him. It had not gone unnoticed among the troopers that this federal agent had a more than professional zeal about this case.

"They want y'all to forget it, huh?"

"Yes." Scanlon nodded. "Tell me, where is that other officer, the one that got off the bridge in time?"

"He's down the hall. Just came in."

He went to the men's locker room and found him awake and eating a sandwich.

"Can I ask you some questions about what happened on the train tracks?" he began, sitting down, taking out a notepad. The officer didn't move.

"Did you see anything clearly about the two people?"

"No."

"What did the other trooper say on the radio?"

"He said there were two fugitives from Florida wanted on federal warrants, and were dangerous."

"Why didn't you close in when they were up on the highway?"

"Shifflett—that's his name—wanted to do it his way."

Scanlon eyed the man. There was something he was not saying.

"His way?"

"To avoid any trouble."

"Trouble?"

The man bit his lip.

"What trouble do you mean?"

"They were discovered in a roadhouse, a gambling place. Some of the boys go there. Everybody does. So, Shiflette couldn't arrest them there. That wouldn't look right."

So that was it. The quarry was lost because the troopers couldn't keep their own fingers out of the till.

"When the train hit their car, did you see it?"

"Are you crazy? I was getting the hell off that bridge."

"No one saw them hit water or come up?"

"No one I know."

Scanlon stood up. He had made his decision.

"Look, I'm going to make you a deal. I could put a warrant on all of you for that gambling house, and we'd find it, wherever it is. But instead, I want you to do something for me."

"What?"

"What's your name?"

"Taggart."

"Okay, Taggart, here's how it is. I want you to find out if anyone has seen those two. Search the area around here. Got that?"

"All the cops around here will be keeping an eye out."

"They don't care, and I don't have any way to make them care. Tell your chief what I said and get on it. Yourself. Understood? Or there will be trouble."

The man stared a moment. Then he nodded.

Reed and Rosalie would not make the sea, for only an hour down-river, the raft struck a rock and came apart, and they barely made it to the bank without getting soaked a second time. Lights on the water, accompanied by a tinkling piano, floated by in the distance, and above them, the stars over Louisiana extended over the bank. From the top, they could see nothing but flat grassland, with no roads, houses, or signs of civilization.

He began to walk, but she stopped him first.

"Just a moment." She put her arms around him. "Do you remember I said you owed me one yesterday?"

He nodded.

"Well, consider it paid." She smiled. "And next time you want to say I love you, try it on the ground, okay?"

In two or three hours, the sky can change enough to be confusing as the stars revolve around the northern star; Orion slowly worked his way from east to west, and by carefully following his direction, they worked their way through the underbrush to harvested fields with dirt paths and tractor roads. They were both very hungry; Rosalie broke the silence.

"You know, they said Moses and Jesus both crossed the desert without food and water for forty days. Can you believe that? How long has it been for us now, two days?"

"Maybe," he answered. "I think there's a certain exhilaration you get after the first pain stops. Suppose we could go that long; think what it would teach you."

She looked at him and laughed.

"Yeah. And we might be hungry for days at this rate."

Sometime, deep into the night, they saw the first lights of man, dimly at first, then crystallizing as the sign and windows of a small, dingy bar on a two-lane asphalt road. A handful of cars was parked outside, and ringing through the night was the sound of a fiddle, guitar, and accordion; as they entered the room, the whoops and hollers of the small but excited crowd hit a crescendo, and the band took a break. They sat in a booth by the door, unsure if they could show themselves. No one came. Minutes went by without their being noticed, and the band began to play again, a fast, pumping melody punctuated by "ya ya ya" from the crowd. A tall, dark man clad in baggy pantaloons and a scarf clasped together at the neck by a stone medallion came to their table and held out his hand to Rosalie, dragging her to her feet. The room grew quiet and tense; Reed began to get up, but she shook her head, laughed, and walked to the floor.

The man danced beautifully, with a natural grace and flamboyant movement, and Rosalie mirrored his motions, their arms extended and touching only at the fingertips as they circled around, her loose hair spinning freely and exciting the crowd. She was laughing as the song ended, and as she started back toward Reed, the man took her hand and swung her into his arms, bending her backward for a deep kiss.

The room cracked silent. She tried to push him away, but he was too strong. Instantly, Reed was on his feet, crossing the floor, but he was blocked by two burly men; he swung hard and sent one reeling and ducked under the other, and the dancer let Rosalie go and stood facing him.

Eye-to-eye they stood; Reed could neither control the man nor lower his own eyes, for that would signal defeat and acceptance. Slowly, they began to move, circling to their left like a pair of prizefighters, pawing the air with their gazes, eyes that flashed with anger and pride, with violence and with power.

From the side, a knife was thrown to the floor, intended to stick by its point between them; Reed reacted perfectly and kicked it away before it stuck. A second and a third were thrown into the ring, and he kicked each one away, denying the trial by knifepoint.

The other man's gaze was burning his; he would have given himself some relief but could not chance the loss of concentration. They continued circling until the man reached out his bare hand, fingers pointing up, offering a test of hand strength to his adversary. Reed slowly reached out and took it and then offered his other hand. They stood in the dingy barroom, locked in hand-to-hand combat, their eyes still burning at each other. Slowly, as if his sight were changing, Reed saw the other man's desire, visualized it in his mind; it was a raft on the great river, and the man was trying to pull upstream, into the current, toward a soft voice he could not see but knew was a woman's. The man was fighting on desire, and Reed knew in an instant how to beat him, those eyes and fingers still locked with his: my love and his desire, he told himself. Love and desire. Where the twain shall meet, desire is blind, and love will find a way. It sounded like soap-opera logic, but it had to work now. If his strength would be tested, he would give it everything.

Staring into the man's eyes, he saw a dim point of light there. Slowly, he expanded it in his concentration, letting it grow, letting it flow and ebb, each time growing brighter at its high point. The tension hung heavy in the smoke and sweat, but Reed concentrated on that point of light. Let it spread, he thought, let it spread far and wide and protect those on whom it shines. The light grew brighter; it seemed overwhelming, but he held on, almost blinded, until at last he cried out a tremendous "Ahhh," and released his adrenaline, bending the man's fingers and bringing him to his knees.

The crowd murmured and shifted its feet, but no one moved; the man in the pantaloons was strong and had a power of his own, and he too yelled and dragged Reed to his knees, still with their eyes locked. Reed told the light to go and return with help; he would hold on. Find me strength, he said to it; find me strength.

❧

James Quisto was thumbing through his scrapbook in New Jersey when he came to an old photograph from Vietnam. It was almost funny until he realized, once again, he knew nothing of Rett's whereabouts since the escape. He did not know if he was alive or under a different name or where he could be. He'd spoken to Lina once, but she knew nothing and assumed he'd left her for good. She had an interesting theory, Quisto thought, that he'd let her go because he had heard once too often that his lack of success was hindering her career. He looked at the photo once again, and there he was: Lakker, the dead man, shot by the ghost of his own violence. He remembered saving his friend from the knifepoint, and he knew Jimmy's rodeo had been a repayment for that.

The chimes in the front room tolled once. What would Rett be doing right now? Probably staring at the sky. He always liked to stare at the sky.

He went out into the front yard and looked up. In Vietnam, the shapes had always seemed strangely alien, like a collection of fairy dragons known by other Vietnamese names. He had been glad to return home and find the sky still held those dippers and warriors he knew. And he began to talk to his friend, wherever he might be.

"May you be free," he whispered. "As the stars wander the sky, may you be free and safe. Wherever you are, I am with you," he said out loud once; then, he said it again. It sent a shiver down his spine, and he went back inside.

⤳

With another tremendous shout, the man overpowered Reed and drove him to the floor, on his belly, still holding on. The stone metal from the man's scarf scraped on the floor; had he mistakenly let the light go? But he raised his head and saw it again, deep in the man's eyes, slowly returning from wherever it had been. He drew on it; he gathered himself up to his knees, and for the first time, his opponent let fear show in his eyes. Reed rose up, forced the man's hands down, down toward the floor, until the pain and the contest had them both shaking fiercely. He got the man down, palms down, and the glistening eyes dropped down also. It was over.

He stood up and released the other man's hands, hands that, by all accounts, should have won. No one in the bar moved until a second tall man walked up and handed him a knife, handle first. He saw the blade reflecting the party lights from the stage—reds, greens, yellows—and he saw himself on the ground, a man in uniform holding him there, with Lakker's hands on his throat.

Lakker, a dead man.

"Kill him, kill him," he heard a whisper.

The loser was now on his knees, waiting.

"Do you speak English?"

"Once in a while," a voice called out. "Do you speak Cajun?"

"We ... don't want anything. Some food. And to be left alone, that's all." He let go of the man's head, but with the knife reached down to the man's scarf, to the stone metal. With the point, he lifted the strands and untied the knot, catching the stone in his hand.

"I will take this."

The man on his knees seemed dazed; another man came over and helped him up. Rosalie came from the corner and buried her face in his shirt, shaking all over. He felt a tap on his shoulder and turned carefully around. It was the Cajun. He held out his hand again palm up, a gesture of friendship, and said something Reed couldn't understand.

"He says he will help you," a nearby man said. "He says he will help you go to wherever you wish to go and will stand by you." There was a pause.

"You can believe him. He is an honest man." The man paused, then continued, "And he won't hit on your woman again."

Reed took the man's hand.

"Please tell him we are grateful for his help."

They were led to a table where two plates of red beans, rice, and smoked meats were waiting for them. They ate quietly, watching the dancers as the band played on, and when they finally danced together, Reed held her tightly in his arms.

Chapter 12

—❦❦❦—

THE RAPPING AT THE DOOR WAS LOUD AND INSISTENT. IT MUST'VE been going on for some time before they heard it.

"Get up!" a voice called out. "We have you a ride west."

They dressed quickly and went outside; there was an old red and white sedan running its motor in the yard. It looked completely out of place amid the scattering chickens.

"Name's Spangler, Spangler Bartone. How y'all doing today? Heard about you two from last night. Pheeyu, wish I'd seen that! Say, what's your names, anyway?"

"Rosalie," she said, breaking the ice.

"Read," he followed suit, shaking hands.

"Well, little lady and Mr. Fella, they tell me you're trying to go west. That right?"

"Yes. Thank you. Where are you going?"

"I'm headed to Arizona myself. And we've got to make time. I have to work there night after tomorrow, so off we go. Got everything?"

They laughed. "Everything we've got."

The cheerful stranger, grinning from ear to ear, looked about thirty and was wearing a white hat with a narrow brim all around, clean blue jeans, and a bright red and white checkered shirt. He looked like a man going to work in the city.

Spangler Bartone reached under the dashboard with his left hand as if feeling for some object. Then he released the handbrake and grabbed the gear shift lever mounted on the steering column. With a muffled jolt, the car eased forward, and he slapped his palm joyfully against the steering wheel.

"Damn, I love to drive this car!"

"What kind of car is this? And where are we?"

"This car? This car is a 1956 Chevrolet Bel Air, the original every-thing, my friend, a wonder of modern man."

"It's very well preserved," chipped in Rosalie, settling into the front seat.

"Damn straight," grinned Spangler.

After a brief silence, Rosalie asked again where they were.

"We are about to leave," he answered. "Just turn around and read this here sign."

They turned and eyed the green sign, bordered with a white stripe. In the middle was a bold splash of white paint.

They drove all day, stopping once for lunch. By nightfall, they were well across Texas, and as it grew dark, they pulled into a campground a couple of miles from the interstate. It had been a long, uneventful day.

They gathered some firewood and built a blaze in the deserted campground; it was fall, and there were no tourists.

Reed took a long shower in the cement block building, and when he emerged, Rosalie was sitting quietly, staring into the flames, watching pieces of ash disappear with the smoke into the night sky.

"Do you think they're still looking for us?"

"I think they'll always be looking for us. We can't ever take anything for granted. Can you handle it?"

She stirred the coals with a long stick.

"I think we'll be all right once we get to Arizona."

He didn't answer.

"And we're alive. Think of it, how easily we might not even be alive. We exist! We might as well go on as if every day counts for something. And it does. Think of it, how different we are from all those people who get up every day and do the same thing all day, every day. We're … free, aren't we?"

"As long as they don't catch us."

"What if they do? If you didn't do anything …"

"I can't prove that."

"Don't they have to prove you did?"

"I can't account for myself. No, this is it. This is our freedom. We're free as long as they don't catch us."

She didn't say anything until he laughed out loud.

"Hey, whatever happened to that guy who used to sit in his apartment and type stories to keep in his drawer?"

She unzipped her jacket and put her hand inside.

"Here," she said. "I bought these for you today." She handed him a ballpoint pen and a small notebook of pressed cardboard, bleached white, with a lavender flower in the upper-left corner. He accepted the present gingerly, as if touching a long-forgotten relic, clicking the pen.

"I suppose you'll drift off into space, won't you? Don't writers do that when they're working?" Her face was luminous in the firelight, her eyes glittering as if deep within each one was a fire all its own.

"I will never be far from you," he said.

"Hey, how y'all doing?" interrupted Spangler Bartone, walking into the firelight with a shiny metal guitar in one hand.

"I've got a tune to learn for a show this week. Want to hear it?"

"Sure," they said.

Spangler sat on the log on Reed's left, cocked back his hat, and started plucking syncopated pairs and trios of notes while sliding a steel bar over the strings with his other hand; when he sang, his voice raw and growly, he tapped his right foot on the dirt.

> Born in a Bel Air
> Born in a Bel Air
> Daddy said, "You're the one"
> Left me standing there
> Long as I live
> Long after I die
> I was born in a Bel Air
> And I know why

'Cause I don't need
None of those white
Hospital room walls
To make me all right
Though my mom is long gone
And my daddy don't care
Till my day is done,
I was born in a Bel Air

Rosalie stopped humming and smiled.

"Wow, that's great. You're really good," said Reed, meaning it.

"You like it? Really? It's my new song." He smiled with genuine pride. "Do you play?"

"No, wish I could, but I never have tried."

"Well, you just wait here a minute." Spangler Bartone grinned, getting up. He went to his car and opened the trunk; after rummaging around for a minute, he returned, bearing a small red guitar with a long rawhide string fastened to each end.

"Here, try this," he said, grinning from ear to ear.

"What do I do now?" Reed asked.

"It's tuned to an open chord. Just strum it. When you get tired of that chord, bar it across the fifth fret like this." He demonstrated with his hand, wrapping the thumb and fingers around the neck and holding it. "Now strum again. See? Different chord. Two more frets up, and you've got the third chord. You can play half the songs ever written with those three."

Read stroked the strings softly; they had a quiet, melodious sound. The fire cracked once, and Rosalie hummed along as she stared into the flames, watching as the sparks flew away like small orange birds into the Texas night.

⚬⁄⚬

There was only one settlement for miles around, so Officer Taggart took a day off and drove there in his own Plymouth, parked discreetly on a side street and went into a coffee shop where a few locals were eating breakfast. He thought he might ask some subtle questions about two people who had disappeared, but he never had to ask. He had only to listen.

He called the private number he'd been given.

"Hello."

"Is this Agent Scanlon?"

"Yes, it is." On the other end, the listener sat upright in his chair.

"This is Taggart. They passed through this town, called something or other, but that doesn't matter. They got a ride with a local guy."

"Where?"

"Arizona."

"That's it?"

"That's it. They left yesterday."

"Wait a minute. How do I know it's the same two people? Anyone describe them to you?"

"It's them. Or it isn't. That's your problem."

"All right, Taggart, you can go. But I want that roadhouse with the casino closed."

Scanlon got to his feet and went down the hallway to a meeting he was not looking forward to, hoping the chief would be too busy to see him. But he wasn't, and he beckoned him to enter.

It was what he expected: he had overstepped his bounds, putting himself in the jail, not informing anyone to back him up and then letting the prisoner escape. Besides, the chief said, there was no hard evidence the man was anything but a vagrant. From now on, he added, the case would be handled by someone else.

Scanlon arrived back in his own office, deeply discouraged, to find one of his associates waiting for him, sitting on his desk.

"Bad news, Bill?" asked Bob Lake, a tall, athletic man with a five-o'clock shadow and a deep voice that always sounded as if he were speaking through a microphone.

"I'm off the Fool case, if that's what you mean."

"I heard that," sympathized the other man, "but listen up: I have a friend in the switchboard who will let us in on anything new that comes in. We haven't lost them yet."

Scanlon studied the other man, with his Nixon-like shadow and too-convincing voice, and wondered what would make his fellow agent take such an interest in this case.

"We, Bob?" he asked quietly.

"Giles was my friend, too," said Lake, swinging his leg back and forth. "It could have been me or you out there getting wasted. We owe it to him to find the guy. And you can use my help."

Scanlon said nothing, thinking it over.

"Come on, Bill, you gotta be realistic."

⨒

On the second day, they sped through Albuquerque, New Mexico's budding desert metropolis, well into the desert of the southwestern states. Spangler Bartone had a singing engagement--"a gig," he called it--at the Grand Canyon Lodge, beginning the next night, and they were making good time. But a plain black car had been one hundred yards behind them for miles, easing unobtrusively down the interstate highway through the late afternoon sunshine. Far away to the right, the burnt green mountains shimmered in the desert air, but Rosalie kept turning and looking over her shoulder, past where Dylan Reed lay across the back seat, threading a strand of rawhide through the small hole in his new stone medallion.

"I wonder where this came from, why it meant anything to him," he mused out loud. "Or to me."

"How'd you end up with it?" Spangler said to the mirror.

"I had to take something to end the fight."

"Okay, I'll buy that."

It was no more than two inches long and barely a quarter-inch thick, and its edges had worn away slightly over the indeterminate years. A circle with two diagonal lines was on one side; on the other, a human stick figure hung down from where the string went through.

"Spangler, is that car following us?" Rosalie asked him.

"I don't know, ma'am. Want me to lose him?"

"Yes."

"My pleasure," he drawled, grinning at the chance to show off his fine car, and soon they were speeding over the sweeping panorama of Western New Mexico, and the black car made no attempt to catch up.

They passed a sign on the right: it said they had crossed the Continental Divide.

"Maybe I'm paranoid." She relaxed, settling back.

"Hell, ma'am, out here, it's not a bad thing to be. You get stranded on one of these roads, you never know who'll turn up, and nearly everybody's got a gun. But you know what else? Out here in all this space, the world sure seems far away. I mean, it's such a big, goddamn huge thing, it's hard to imagine getting all wrapped up in those little bitty cares you get back east. Least that how it's always seemed to me. Want to hear a little theory of mine?"

"Sure."

"If you go to South America or Australia, the water in a toilet bowl flows down the hole backward. I mean, it spirals in the opposite direction than on this side of the equator. It's a whole different thing. Now, we're across the Continental Divide, and all the water that was flowing eastward to the Atlantic is going to be flowin' west, toward the Pacific Ocean. It's mighty dry in these parts, but the plain fact is that water acts just the opposite here than back east. That's right, isn't it?"

"Okay."

"Your body—mine too—is, what, 98 percent water, something like that? Now, don't you think that kind of difference would affect the way we are? I mean, we don't have any way to measure, but the plain fact is, I come out here every so often and I feel different, like all the life of me wants to go in a different direction. Then you realize what a precious commodity water is out here—man, you get caught out in this desert, and you'll die for water. Shit, there ain't no gold worth a glass of water at the right time. You learn to follow the water out here, build your whole life around that water, 'cause if you don't, you ain't goin' to live long enough to watch the sun go down in this heat. Now back where I live, in Loosiana, we got so damn much water you can't stand the smell of it half the time, you know what I mean?" And he laughed once out loud, slapping the steering wheel with his palm.

Around sundown, they turned off the interstate onto a two-lane road, up a long, slow grade toward a vast rock with a huge cleft in it, right where the highway cut through.

"Dig this," Spangler said, slowing the car. They shot through the opening, and all three gasped as the vast panorama of Arizona sprang up before their eyes, a vista extending miles into the desert. Before long, the first bright stars twinkled in the darkening sky, while far off in the west rode the thin, fading crimson line that was all that remained of the day. In its last glow, the land stood shimmering before them, its seemingly barren landscape stretching off into the future with only the slender black stripe of highway to follow. They drifted quietly along the highway for two more hours, only rarely passing any signs of habitation: a store here, a small house there. Slowly the night enveloped them in its deep, mystical emptiness, until, at last, Rosalie spotted a small motel and restaurant ahead.

"Here, Spangler," she said as it passed. And he pulled off into the dirt.

It took a minute to say goodbye to their new friend, who stood waiting as they pulled out blankets and food Rosalie had stashed in the trunk.

"Got a good woman there." He grinned at Reed. "Takes care of business."

"So long. I hope we can come hear you sing somewhere," Reed said as they shook hands.

"Any time," Spangler answered, accepting her kiss on his cheek with a wink. They stood watching his taillights trail down the road.

They looked around. There were a few cars at the motel and restaurant, fifty yards back; otherwise, it was open land in every direction.

"Come on," said Rosalie, taking his hand. They walked quickly through the weathered pine trees, away from the highway. Silent, they had walked a few hundred yards from the highway when the earth yawned before them into a giant canyon, a place where stone and dirt seem to have been carved by a great ocean too long ago for anything but the earth itself to remember. They stood, holding hands, for a long quiet time.

Rosalie let go of him and went along the rim, looking for something. Finally, she found it, a wall where handholds had been worked into the rock, making it possible to descend into the dark recess of earth.

"You've been here before," he said.

She grinned back.

"You've guessed my secret. Come on."

She led him down the handholds to where the sandstone had formed a cave beneath the canyon rim. Eaten away by wind and water, a large pile of rocks concealed the opening.

He set their meager belongings on the ground and sat down. Rosalie stood and watched the sky.

"Aren't you tired?" he asked.

She didn't answer him at first, and he lay back and closed his eyes, weary from their journey. He did not notice how alive Rosalie felt and barely heard her before he fell asleep.

"You know," she mused, "this is a magical place."

⁂

In Chicago, Scanlon's private obsession had led him to Lina, hoping to learn where the man he knew as Rett Haskins might have gone. And now he waited in a small restaurant for the lovely blonde woman whose picture he had seen once; he could have had her subpoenaed, he had hinted, but would rather just meet and talk.

Finally, she arrived, alone and dressed as if this were a quiet romantic rendezvous with a lover, her face hidden beneath a wide-brimmed hat, her curves outlined in the simple top and skirt.

"Let's get one thing straight right off," she said. "I haven't heard from him since he went east. For a while, I waited. Then I was living with

another man, and he called—at least I think it was him. The other guy
answered the phone. We split up, too; my love life's not much to talk
about, I guess."

Scanlon looked her over and found that hard to believe.

"Anyway, I don't know who he knows out there. He never mentioned
anyone to me. He had a friend in New Jersey, a Quest or something like
that. We're finished, I'm sure. By now he's probably traveling with some
redhead."

"That's true," he assured her. They had some dinner and some wine,
and Scanlon discovered he liked this woman very much. Later, when he
drove her home, she surprised him and invited him in for a nightcap.
She brought him his drink, and he summoned up all his nerve, put his
hand on her waist and drew her toward him.

She put her arms around him and kissed him back, and soon he was
kissing her breasts in a room lit only by the moon. He did not know if he
was revenging himself on the man who had stolen his own wife's heart,
but as he held her in his arms, he knew it felt so good to make love again.

❧

"You're awake," Rosalie said matter-of-factly. "Are you hungry?"

He turned and saw her a few feet away, standing at the edge of the
cave. She had her hair down and was wearing a thick black jersey that
hung snugly down to her thighs. In her hand, she held up a can of tuna
fish.

"Lunch," she grinned. "Sleep well?"

He shook his head to clear his mind.

"What was that you said last night?" he asked.

She clasped her hands together, remembering.

"I said this is a magical place. Why?"

"Why did you bring us here?"

"Well, I don't know. I knew we'd be safe. I know a few people here
that might help us."

"You do?"

"Yes. I was a student here a few years ago on a cultural exchange program. I lived with a family in a town near here." She dug out the tuna and spread it over two slices of dry bread.

"But why did we come here, to this canyon?"

She looked at him for a few seconds before answering, as if she too wanted to understand.

"I found this place once when I went walking by myself," she said. "Then I came back a few times, even camped out here alone. I dreamed a few times that I was a baby tossed into the water, and sometimes that I lived beside a spring. For some reason, this place feels as if I've always belonged here." She looked out over the canyon, down a steep angle from the front of the cave, where a sandy beach gave way to a narrow, flat stretch of dry ground that receded into the distance.

"That was a few years ago. But we can stay here until it's safe to go somewhere else."

He looked around at their new home. There was the unmistakable cool dampness of water on the inside back wall and that pile of soft rock across the open front. It looked as if the overhanging roof might come crashing down at any time as the spring seeped its way through the stone.

"How often," he asked, "do you suppose this roof caves in?"

She walked over with the tuna fish.

"Once in a while. Every few years, probably. I guess it's a matter of timing."

He slid his hand along the inside of her leg.

"Nice dress," he whispered, drawing her toward him. "Think it's gonna cave in today?"

"Eat some food." She laughed and sat down, handing him some bread and a fork. "And be serious."

"There is a spring here," she continued, passing him the can, "so it does cave in sometimes, here in front. You know, in older times, people came to the spring for guidance, and there was a keeper—maybe even an oracle--who lived there beside it."

He chewed slowly, leaning back against a broken chunk of stone.

"You think that was yourself?" he asked.

"No, of course not. Well, I don't know. This place reminds me of something else, as if it was once covered, like a huge cave at the edge of the sea."

She watched him eat.

"Have you ever read Plato?"

"Right now, it escapes me," he confessed.

"Plato supposedly was initiated by Egyptian magicians, who sent him into a great cave. The only way out was to jump off a cliff inside the cave, in total darkness, trusting in fate. You would land in the river flowing out, of course. It was a symbolic death/rebirth ritual, but it required a river to be flowing out, which meant a spring somewhere."

He chewed more slowly.

"And you showed the way, down those handholds," he said, pointing toward the near cliff. The canyon stretched out below them, as if once, long ago, this great hole beside this tiny spring was full of water.

"But this isn't Egypt," he protested.

"It's more ancient than that," she answered. "You want to know why I brought you here? To see this ancient world, that's why. Look around—you don't see this kind of permanence anywhere back east. This place is old, timeless." She drew her legs under her and squinted, looking deep into the sunlight. He reached toward her, but she stood abruptly.

"Not now, okay?" she said. "I want to be alone for a while."

Later, as night fell, a bright moon lit the starry sky, and in the crisp air, she led him back up the handholds to the rim of the canyon.

"In one of my dreams," she began, sitting down a foot from the edge, "I was living here alone while below us was a great city. Then, one day, I found this place. I stayed until it was dark—the moon was full, like tonight—and I had a vision. Look over there. See that? That large rock? It's the head of a pharaoh. I saw planes taking off way over there, where that shelf of rock is. And down there, that's the City of Light, where that wall of columns is."

"The what?" he asked, sitting next to her.

"The City of Light—that's what I call it. The people who've lived here since long ago say that when the twins, the North and South Pole, left their homes and moved, the sea left this canyon. That's the old legends. But you can see it was real, can't you?"

He looked out across the dim expanse of dirt, stone, and moonlight; at first, it did not speak. And then, before his eyes, the shadows began to move. Faces appeared as light carved its way upwards from the great depth below, and the whole canyon became a living world, just as she had described. What had been a pile of rocks in the distance became a glowing presence in the desert night, and, in one instant, he saw it all: the great civilizations, the great dreams they had, the great illusions, the piles and piles of sand they had become.

"There's one thing that really pisses me off," Rosalie said. He drifted back from his reverie. "That light over there, I feel like it's watching us."

His eyes followed the direction she pointed: off in the distance, on the far rim of the cliffs to the east, was a bright red light, standing eerily on a tall, spindly tower like the eye of a giant insect.

"It's said there are places on the earth with real magic, where a magician can travel to and from by going through the earth. Doesn't something like that make you wonder?"

"Maybe it's to keep planes from crashing," he answered.

"I don't know," she said, looking off toward the northern sky, where the farthest cliffs extended out into the open desert. "Sometimes, I think there are people who just can't stand natural beauty. Show them something made perfect, and they pave it or put up something ugly just for the sake of it. Or worse, they try to use the energy of the place like this for themselves."

"Do you really believe that?"

She turned and faced him.

"I believe in real magic," she said. "Don't you? Don't you think your life is telling you that?"

He shrugged.

"I don't know. I can't explain it all so easily."

She smiled as her eyes danced with the moonlight.

"Take it from me," she said, "you're a very magical man."

They sat and watched the canyon glimmer for a long time. At length,

Reed saw the head of an eagle silhouetted against the full moon, as if it had been carved there by some long-forgotten artist.

"Rosalie, this place is incredible," he said softly, "but I don't think we can spend the winter here."

"We can go see my friend Michael. He'll help us."

"Okay," he said.

"Well, not right now." She giggled, nuzzling him, and began unbuttoning his shirt. Soon they had undressed, and she was on top of him, making love at the edge of the canyon. As she arched her back and leaned away, he looked up between her breasts straight into the full moon, and her whole body seemed to glow. She took him in the moonlight as he held onto the dirt with his fingers to keep from going over the edge.

Chapter 13

———⟞ʘⳚʘ⟝———

THE DOOR WAS OPENED BY A SHORT MIDDLE-AGED MAN IN A RED AND white checkered shirt. He had jet-black hair pulled back into a ponytail behind a well-baked face. Squinting into the night air, he looked like a man who had just been reading under a bright light.

"Hello, Michael," she said.

His gaze went from one to the other and back.

"Rosalie."

He said it as if he were trying to convince himself.

"May we come in?"

"Of course."

They stepped quickly into the house. Inside, it was dim and sparsely furnished, with a table, chairs, and a typewriter in view. In the corner, beside a stuffed chair, a small lamp filled the room with the odor of burning oil.

"Michael, this is Dylan Reed. And this is Michael Lanaka. Reed is also a student of Geller's, Michael," she finished.

The two men shook hands; the older one nodded but did not make eye contact.

"Ah, Geller," he mused. "And how is he?"

"He died this summer. I'm sorry. I would have written, but there was no time."

He studied them carefully before speaking again.

"You have come on foot? I heard no car," he said.

"We walked here from nearby. We're in trouble and need some help," she said.

The Indian man's eyes narrowed.

"What trouble?"

She didn't answer.

"The police are looking for us. There was a murder, and the police believe I did it," Reed answered for her.

"Did you do it?" The man challenged him.

"No."

Lanaka sighed heavily.

"But you are fugitives." It was a quiet statement of fact.

"We need somewhere to hide, yes," Rosalie said quietly, sitting down on a nearby chair. Michael lowered his eyes and walked over to the window. He stared deep into the darkness outside for a moment, then turned to face them.

"How rude of me." He shrugged. "You must be very hungry. Why don't you sit down while I bring you something to eat?"

"Thank you," exhaled Rosalie with relief. She looked at Reed, and they sat at the simple wooden table as their host went to the rear of the house. Reed spied the newspaper lying by the typewriter, where Michael had left it. On the front page, above the large caption, "The American Guerillas," was a grainy photograph of two people in midair, just below the open door of a car. In the background was the hazily focused gridwork of a railroad bridge.

"The search for the Fool, as he is known, fleeing from a federal murder charge in Connecticut, turned dramatically southward yesterday. Now traveling under the name Dylan Reed, the fugitive and his lawyer, Rosalie Lenoir, barely eluded a predawn police roadblock at the Mississippi River, taking the plunge into the Big Muddy instead. One patrolman was killed in the chase. A police spokesman said, 'They won the battle today, but the war's not over yet.'"

Lanaka returned with three plates, forks, knives, a large melon, and a skillet full of fried potatoes.

"You read the *New York Post?*" Rosalie asked.

"I was in New York four days ago for a speech in a cultural center," he replied. "Some friends pointed that out to me. Friends of yours and Geller's, I believe."

He sat down and cut each of them a slice of melon, then spooned some potatoes onto each plate. He passed them across the table to his guests. Reed bit slowly into the sweet, wet fruit, deciding to make it last as long as possible.

"I do not know what it is you are running from," Lanaka began. "But this is a dangerous time. There are people here trying to prevent your government from stealing our land for a mining company. People say there are informers in the villages, government informers. If they find you here, they will use this information."

They did not interrupt him as he speared a slice of potato and continued.

"I have learned there is a difference between your people and mine. Your people do not know where to stop. You dig up everything to have more dollars, until there is no more land for the Creator. Then you begin moving the people from their homes, and all the dollars, which the people are told will make their lives better, are spent instead on police, until we are all prisoners."

They did not interrupt.

"And when the land is violated," he concluded, "the Creator will lay his hand on this world, as He has done before. There will be a terrible time then, a true test of man's faith. It has all been written."

Reed sat, motionless, chewing the melon, and swallowed it down with some deliberation.

"Has it really?" he mused quietly. The Indian looked up from his plate.

"What do you ask?"

"Has it really all been written," he repeated, not bothering to make it a question.

Lanaka chewed his food patiently, a man in no hurry. At last, not sure if the question was sarcastic or merely polite, he went on.

"There are events that must take place. You people are very greedy, hungry for a fulfillment you do not have, afraid to seek it from the only source that matters. Instead, you try to build it with machines, to buy it with dollars. And so, your government has made a tribal council that has taken dollars for a mining lease. With this, they have bought police cars and uniforms.

"Police," he spat the word. "For generations, we've needed no one. For this, you take the Creator's land. And so I say, it is not safe for you here."

Reed looked over at Rosalie, who stared downcast at her plate, ignoring the fried potatoes.

"You know," Reed said, "I think it would help if you stopped referring to us as 'you people.' We didn't come here as part of the government. We are no more in its favor than yourself. We came here looking for a friend to help us. If you want us to leave, fine. But you can stop treating us as your enemy."

He had finished the melon: only the skin remained. Lanaka reached out and cut him another, shoving it gently toward him with a smile.

"Perhaps," he answered, "you will learn who your people truly are."

Reed leaned forward and reached for the fruit, the medallion swinging loosely out from beneath his open collar. His host's eyes narrowed momentarily, as they studied the suspended stone, then came up to Reed's. They had seconds, as he watched them, chewing in silence until the calloused old fingers held a slender rind.

"There is someone I want you to meet," Lanaka said at last, and bit into the last slice. "Are you ready to go?"

The night was lit by a golden harvest moon as they set off on the dirt path across the grassy plain. In the distance, a great rock, hundreds of feet high, flat on top, sticking straight up from the desert floor, looked like a shadow under its light. Lanaka moved quickly through the grass, making no sound. Somewhere in the distance, a dog was howling; a car engine started and drove off, feeding its harsh melody like a phonograph record. They followed through the grass behind him, brushing it with their legs and arms at first, then getting the groove that would slip them through quietly. At last, they stopped for a breather. Lanaka wasn't even tired from the brisk pace he set.

"Be silent," he whispered. "The night will speak to us."

Seated on the cool dirt, they caught their breath as a large bee buzzed by, and then there was quiet, an absence of noise—no breeze, no animal sounds, no hum of city streets, that nothing that is something by being itself: silence.

Minutes later, deep into their reveries, a low droning hum began to intrude from afar. Slowly, it grew louder, until headlights appeared some distance away, then turned to Lanaka's house. They could not see without standing, but he motioned, palms down, to stay put.

A spotlight beam zoomed over their heads, circled their position, and went away. Doors closed, the car left, its occupant satisfied no one was around. They stood up quickly and squinted across the plane as the car sped away.

"Tribal police," he said quietly. "Probably looking for you."

Soon, they arrived at the base of a wall of rock ascending skyward, and they began climbing a steep but well-worn trail, switching back and forth on itself, step-by-step toward the stars. At last, they reached a small village, its houses of baked mud bolstered by the occasional wooden plank, built in rows on top of each other like a tiny urban neighborhood perched high above the uninhabited desert. Lanaka led them to a doorway and tapped softly. An old woman appeared behind a pane of dirty, streaked glass, her long gray hair tied back to accentuate her copper-colored face. Without a word, she led them into a back room, lit by a single oil lamp.

A very old man sat on a wooden chair, listening to their approach. He arched his neck and circled his head once on it like a bird on a branch. But he did not look at them, for the eyes in the wrinkled old face were blind.

Lanaka spoke quickly, in a strange tongue. He beckoned them forward, placing his hand on Reed's shoulder, forcing him down to his knees, facing the old man.

The ancient eyes looked through him, far beyond him but not at him. He raised an arm, slowly, with some difficulty, and rested his hand on Reed's shoulder. Then, lightly framing the sides of his face, he tapped his chin with a fingernail. He found the strand of rawhide and traced it across his neck until he found the medallion. He placed both hands on it, holding it gently in his fingers as he divined the carvings on its sides with his bent fingers. He took a deep breath, sat up straight, and listened to something far, far away. Then he exhaled a long, deep note, like a low breeze, and let it go.

Michael helped Reed to his feet. He led him and Rosalie back out of the room and into another dimly lit area, motioning toward a couch and chair.

"It's very late," he said. "Why don't you go ahead and sleep. You are safe here tonight."

Tired after the long walk and climb, they complied gratefully, holding each other on the long couch. But when he awoke, Reed was alone. He got up and walked through the house, ending up outside; the sun wasn't up, but it was becoming light. A rooster announced itself, and he stretched his muscles to wake up.

Slowly, his eyes adjusted to the view. Standing in front of the old house, he looked beyond the rock's end over a great plane of dirt, where, far below in the distance, a faraway automobile was no more than a moving dot. Overhead, a few clouds floated like three-dimensional balloons above him, but not that high above him, as the sun, immense and vibrating at the horizon, slowly peeled itself off the flaming sand and, as if by sheer force of will, ripped itself free of the horizon.

Just as it cleared, he heard Michael Lanaka speak behind him.

"First, purple, then yellow light of morning, then a red ball, and then yellow again. A man has these colors, it is said; then he loses them in the heat of life and must return to the desert to regain them with his death."

Reed stood there, profoundly moved by what he had seen. At last, he stirred himself.

"Have you seen Rosalie?" he asked.

The man squinted at the yellow sun. He turned his head slowly, like a cat eyeing an intruder, then reached into the pocket of his red and white checkered shirt.

"Here," he said, and handed Reed a note:

Reed,

Well, we have to be apart now. I love you.

Rosalie

He had to read it three times before it registered.

Chapter 14

—⟨⟩⟨⟩⟨⟩—

"**W**HAT DOES THIS MEAN?"

"What does it say?"

"It says, 'We have to be apart now.'"

"It must mean what it says."

His calm was unnerving.

"She wouldn't just leave. Is this some kind of trick? When did she give this to you? Where was she going?" Reed demanded heatedly.

Michael Lanaka put his hands in his trouser pockets and raised his eyes to the sky.

"It's no trick," he said. "She has gone. You had better calm down and collect yourself."

He kicked the dirt like a horse scraping its hooves.

"It doesn't make sense. Why would she do that?" He took a long, slow breath and softened his tone as the quiet Indian said nothing.

"What does 'have to be apart' mean?' Has someone, yourself perhaps, made her go somewhere?"

"No. Wherever she went, it was her choice."

"Do you know where she is?"

It was a question met by silence and a quiet penetrating stare. After a few seconds, Dylan Reed looked down as his still-pawing foot dislodged a small stone. He bent down and picked it up, straightened, and fired it through the glass pane of the wooden door, shattering the glass and making a large gong when it hit metal inside.

"You had better control your temper," Lanaka said.

"If you don't tell me where she is, I'm going to throw you through that door."

"Yes. Don't white men always resort to violence to get their way? Why don't you go back where you belong?" Lanaka turned his back on him, facing the sun once more. There was a faint breeze drifting over the mesa top, and a shingle banged somewhere not far away.

Rosalie had come into his life so suddenly and been with him so constantly since that he had come to expect it, to accept it, to see it as the natural state of affairs—from habit? Love? Need? Accident? It was inconceivable to him that she could simply leave, freely, without a word.

"For now," she had written. They had fled police, run for their lives, fought, driven, sung, made magic, and made love together without knowing where it would end; but that she might up and leave, just vanish, had not occurred to him at all. Was it possible? Could it be true? Didn't she love him too, want to be with him? The thought of this possibility made him shiver, as if an electric current had shot up his back. He kept his eyes level with the man in the checkered shirt, who did not return his stare or speak.

And what of the note? Was it really a farewell? Was it written under duress, to throw him off? Or a clue? He still held the note in his left hand, but he did not look at it.

Or was it a goodbye note, simply that, left by someone who, for reasons of her own, preferred a quick, easy exit, no messy scene, just gone one morning, "I love you" thrown in as a parting gift?

Michael made no attempt to leave, maintaining his calm, slightly awakened gaze, sniffing the cool breeze, the November air getting chillier every morning. Reed looked at that quiet gaze, the deep black eyes, and, forcing himself to relax, he fell outwardly into the same rhythm of breath as the Indian man. He could do nothing but return the silence and wait.

He held the note, all he had of her now, with the fingers of both hands. As if he had switched himself back on, Lanaka blinked, inhaled quickly, then relaxed, amusement creasing the sunbaked skin around the opaque black pools through which he studied the white man before him.

"The sword of love has two edges, don't you think?" he pronounced in a soft voice, nodding his head. He slapped Reed on the shoulder and smiled wistfully, then went on to his point.

"Ah, my friend, I'm sorry for you," Lanaka said, and stepped abruptly past the blond-haired, blue-eyed man in the denim jacket, leaving him staring out at a horizon of blue sky and desert, miles away and hundreds of feet below. In the dirt street, Reed now stood alone.

The door banged shut behind him.

෴

There is, in a small village, a routine of life that no outsider can fathom immediately. The willingness of people living close together to stay out of each other's way, an attunement to the weather and the passing of seasons—these are the basics of the simple life. So it was that the population of the small mesa-top town awoke and went about its business gathering food for winter, repairing its dwellings, and living through another day in the high desert, without visibly concerning itself with the quiet white man seated on the ground, his back against the old house, sitting there hour after hour. They did not know him. Nor did they realize he was at that moment locked in one of the greatest struggles of his life, the one within himself.

Should he wait? Was there no prospect of her return? Should he go? To where? He had no home, no place dear to his heart, no place where he could be left alone, no place at all that mattered to him. In the face of what he had lost, that he was a wanted man receded from his thoughts, and, unafraid of capture, he sat quietly through the hours, knowing that any motion on his part might take him farther from where she might find him, if she wanted to. Did she want to find him? Had he no faith in her love? He remembered, countless times, her touch, the look in her eyes, her words; and yet the incontrovertible fact was she had gone, leaving nothing but a few words of goodbye.

The day dragged on, and for much of it the sun shone directly above. By late afternoon, he was in the shade, and the chill breeze of autumn began to wear him down. At last, he got up, stood before the house, and prepared to enter: for water, for warmth, for what? He turned from the door, the place where he had been asleep only that morning. Slowly, as if in a daze, he walked through the dirt streets of the village, absorbing the dismal smell of livestock and the muskiness of mud baking in the sun all day long. At the bend was an old woman staring from her doorway. He stopped and smiled at her.

"May I have some water?" he asked her, his voice unused for hours, croaking hoarsely.

The woman receded into her house. A moment later, she returned with a glass of water. She was old and wrinkled, her baked skin the victim of her desert lifetime, but her black eyes shone with curiosity beneath the thatch of white hair on her head.

He took the water and drank it gratefully; she stood there, watching him.

"Thank you," he gasped when he had finished. She nodded in silence.

"I'm looking for someone," he began. "A white woman, with long red hair. Have you seen her?" And he illustrated the long hair with his hand.

The old woman shook her head.

"Do you understand me?" he asked.

Again she frowned and shook her head, then took the glass and held it up, asking in her way if he wanted more.

"No, thank you," he said and smiled. She shrugged and turned to leave, then stopped when he spoke again.

"Where am I?" he asked.

She pointed to a gap in the houses, through which there was a crude path; then, she went back inside. He watched her vanish into the brown dwelling, all patched together of concrete block, boards, and mud, and he shivered.

The path led between the houses to the south rim of the town, then descended toward the desert. He followed it down, winding his way through the rocks and dirt; twice, he passed small groups of Indians on their way up, but they ignored him and walked by.

At the bottom, a spring spilled from the rock into a small, rectangular wood and stone pool, from which the villagers drew their water through a worn-looking faucet of dark brass. He had another drink there, cupping the cold precious liquid into his hand. There was no one around. They had left him alone all day, alone with himself, as if they were not involved. He kicked the side of the pool, angry, frustrated; the water shimmered with his violence but told him nothing.

It was getting late. The sun was lower in the sky than the ramshackle outhouses perched along the rock's ledges, their droppings streaking the sides of the great rock with multicolored bands of human excrement. The sun itself, a red, throbbing thing, hung just above the horizon as Dylan Reed looked straight into it, squinted, and focused his eyes.

"All right," he said out loud. "I'll go. But I will be back."

Abruptly, he turned, slipping into the tall grass and scrub pine, disappearing into the desert.

Chapter 15

———⟨ʘ/ʘ/ʘ⟩———

ITOOK HIM MOST OF THE NIGHT TO FIND THE CAVE, TAKING CARE HE was not followed, avoiding people. At last, the desert opened, and he climbed down the handholds into the canyon they had shared. Their belongings were untouched; if anyone else knew of the place, they had not been there. Nor, apparently, had she. The blankets and food she had bought and stored were intact: a few cans of soup and tuna fish, two gallons of water, some bread and cheese, a knife, matches, paper, a can opener, spoons, forks and plates. He opened a can of tuna and ate from the can, dipping the bread in the oil when he had finished. Just before daylight, he slept, alone for the first time in weeks. The large red bulb across the canyon, its sinister eye staring relentlessly out from high atop its spidery legs, was his only companion.

When he awoke, it was almost dark; the scarlet clouds were fading into the deep blue space that would become the night sky. He ate some more bread and made a small fire, pocketing the matches, but before long, he became restless and unable to sit and think any longer, and he put it out.

Making his way up the handholds, he climbed to the high desert and set out on the road back to the village. After some distance, he heard dogs barking, picking up his scent, and he circled around their sound until the barking eased off. Several minutes later, he came to a few small shacks packed squalidly together; beside them, a line of outhouses perched on the edge of the great rock. There appeared to be no one around. He ran to the side of a house, scaled a ladder leaning against the wall, and quickly was on the roof of the pueblo dwelling, two stories above the dirt streets. A large bird squawked at him, then shifted its weight irritably, chained by its ankle to the rooftop. From his vantage point, he could see most of the town, its street winding in off the highway, making a drunken S through the clusters of sunbaked mud-and-board houses, then circling around on itself like a great snake eating its own tail so that the main portion of the houses was within the loop. All of them, built on top of the great rock, seemed to float in the air above the vast desert plain that receded into the obscurity of the night; it was as if he were atop a flying carpet suspended in midair.

Dylan Reed sat down and began his vigil, watching the seemingly lifeless town. As if for the first time, he began to collect the observations that had nearly passed him by: the absence of power lines, the silence of a place where electricity did not hum. Whatever the people of the village did at night, they clearly did not, unlike the rest of America, sit in front of a television set. There were no streetlights, and the house windows, covered by boards, cardboard, cloth, or glass to keep out the dust, were dark.

A door opened, and a young woman left a nearby house. She walked out to a station wagon parked in front, got in, and turned the key. But she did not start the engine; instead, she twisted the radio dial until she found what she wanted and cranked up the music into a pulsating, metallic noise, as if the entire car were a speaker. Within seconds, other doors opened as other younger Indians walked out to the automobile; and then there was dancing, cigarettes, laughter, and a dozen young voices singing for the whole village to hear:

> And I wonder, still I wonder,
> Who'll stop the rain?

Right after the song ended, a man came outside, walked to the car, and switched off the key. The kids complained briefly, but to no avail, and soon, they returned to their houses. In a few seconds, the street was quiet again save for a lone voice trailing off, singing, "Who'll stop the rain?" from inside a house somewhere.

The moon rose higher in the sky. A slight breeze, chilly and lonesome, forced Reed to button his jacket and hunker down against the rooftop. But he stayed on, watching, learning the routine of the small village until the quiet night had virtually seduced him into its dreamlike state and the first stirrings of activity passed him by, almost unnoticed. One by one, emerging silently from their homes, a group of men formed in the street, their chests bare, their faces in blue and yellow luminescent paint that took on an eerie glow in the moonlight. Without speaking or hurrying, each walked the dirt street around to the far end of the loop, where a slender trail split off to make its way down the side of the rock to the spring below. They turned onto the trail, disappearing from Reed's sight behind the last of the houses.

He scrambled down from his perch and followed them, carefully staying out of sight. There were no others on the street. He reached the trail and moved stealthily along it until he had cleared the houses. There was nothing but the cliff edge and the great desert ahead. A crisp sound caught his ear; he dropped to the ground and spotted a lone Indian lighting a cigarette a few yards away. Motionless, Reed watched as the man smoked nonchalantly, staring absently into the starry heavens, apparently unaware of his presence. After a few seconds, a voice spoke as if from the ground itself; the smoker stood up straight and pointed at the sky, and as Reed followed the direction of his arm, he saw the bright stars of Orion overhead in the autumn sky. Of the other voice, all he could see were two long, antenna-like projections sticking up from the ground, and just as strangely as they had come, they vanished again. The first man, unpainted and wearing a shirt, continued his cigarette.

Something, or someone, was down there. Reed studied the terrain: They were near the edge of the giant rock on which the village was built, in a spot that seemed made of flat-topped stone, a few yards from the nearest house.

He crawled back along the trail, taking care to remain unseen. A few steps brought him to the edge of a dwelling, where he scooped some small stones into his hand. He took aim on the man nearby, who had just dropped his cigarette and crushed it with his foot; the first stone missed, but the second caught him on the chest. Staggering slightly, the man looked around, seeing nothing. He stood still for a moment, then succumbed to his curiosity and went looking for whoever had launched the stone. Reed had only a moment, but it was enough to let him pass, find the hole, grab onto a rope ladder, and climb well down the three-foot square shaft into the earth before the guard had returned to his post.

With a soft thud, he landed on the cool dirt. He was in a large underground chamber, lit by the weaving flicker of a fire pit some thirty feet away. Quickly, he sneaked in the other direction and settled against a wall of earth, in the darkest corner of the room.

The men he had followed were seated before the fire, their backs to him. Another man, wearing a headdress with two long, antelope-like antlers fixed crookedly on top of his head, was singing the moaning, cascading melody of an ancient ritual song, his eyes closed in rapture. On and on he sang, neither hurrying nor laboring for breath, chanting the seemingly formless words to the fire and the silence, a spell punctuated occasionally by the resonant answering moan of his listeners, as if the song had touched some deep chord within themselves. The minutes went by until Reed, too, was taken into the hypnotic mood of the song, lifted into his inner self, not even noticing the deep sighs he was exhaling into the darkness.

And then, without warning, the singer began speaking in English:

"Tonight, you will meet the Intruder, for he is with us. He is clever. He is ruthless. He is without fear, yet he brings it wherever he goes. He is light, for even evil is light at the core of its evil shell; yet, he will cast the world into darkness. And when this happens, you must rise up and free yourself into the light above or perish. And if you perish, the Intruder will grind your soul into the dust with his heel, for this is his nature. And it will be as if you never existed. But if you are swift, you will arise and escape him, and then you will never fear him again in this or any other time."

Again, the old man took up his song, moaning into every corner of the room.

As if from nowhere, another form materialized at the foot of the entrance shaft, a glistening black shape, twisting and writhing on two spindly legs. It whirled and faced Reed, looking directly into the lightless space in which he sat, his catlike eyes glowing from within, a white star painted on the center of his forehead.

Their eyes met for a moment, and Dylan Reed thought he had been discovered. But when he blinked, the black shape had gone, leaping in two bounds to the fire pit, where he faced the seated group with a smooth, spidery dance, his arms rising and falling in a Kali-like weave, his bare feet stepping alternately with the piston rotation of his hands and arms, all arms and legs, as if he had several of each. Then, hissing audibly, he spat once into the fire; instantly, it vanished, plunging the lower world into total darkness.

There was a bedlam of bodies slamming into each other as everyone made for the air shaft. Reed, jolted from his reverie, stayed seated, waiting, as a sweaty body bounced against his shoulder in the dark. He reacted instinctively with an elbow that hit somewhere; but no words were spoken, just the moans and grunts of men groping their way through one small opening toward the stars above.

One by one, they ascended to the plateau above them, climbing the rope ladder from the depths of the earth toward the three bright stars of Orion's belt in the heavens. And as each head popped from the ground, freeing itself from the prison of darkness below, two men welcomed the new arrival with a pailful of the desert's most precious commodity: cold, shocking water. One after another they came, until the old two-horned priest, who had seen it all countless times before and had waited patiently below until the others had arisen, was there on the plateau also.

Taking a quick count, he saw there was one pail of water left. Soon, he would be allowed to eat a meal for the first time in three days; but this was the time he relished, the completion of the year's cycle, when the new young men were welcomed into the ancient ways of his people, a line stretching back to antiquity, to the very spirits themselves. Even the chilly night air, winter closing fast on its heels, could not dampen the exhilaration he felt at this time as he sat on his haunches to await the last initiate.

Deep inside the earth, the muffled sounds of escaping bodies had given way to an orderly procession, then to jubilant voices in the distance. The absence of light joined with a total lack of sound to produce a deep, black void, in which sat Dylan Reed, a stranger from the world above. Lost in thought, no closer to Rosalie than a day ago, he remained motionless for a time, as if the subterranean emptiness had freed him from the necessity of action and brought him the clarity of perception that is only possible when the world has ground to a halt. Hearing himself breathe, seeing himself surrounded in darkness, he realized consciously, for the first time since Rosalie had left, the torment of his own mind, the anxiety of his thoughts, the tension of his body, and he sank into the cool, embracing dirt of the wall behind him, slowing his breathing, feeling once again the life stirring in his soul. After weeks of running and escapes, only to lose the one part of his world that was truly precious to him, he had literally dropped out of sight into the very bowels of the earth. From here, there was, in every way, nowhere to go but up.

At last, the cold dirt and his cramped position forced him to stand. He rose and stepped carefully across the chamber floor, stretching his hands before him. But the large room was now in total blackness, and he felt and saw nothing that could guide him. Even the fire pit, once bright enough to light the ceremony, had completely vanished.

Suddenly, as if it had crossed the room to meet him, he blundered into something, and he heard the distinct sound of wooden objects colliding, as whatever he had hit fell away. Reaching into his pocket, he retrieved the matches and lit one; he had crossed the chamber and reached the altar, for there at his feet lay several long, cylindrical flutes, their attached feathers splayed out on the dirt. Against the nearby wall were a few grotesque masks, fixed on staffs summed into the ground. Silent, he contemplated the religious artifacts that expressed countless generations of worship: red, blue, green, yellow, the faces of snakes, great birds, and fierce gods stood watch over this ancient tribe's prayers, shepherding its way through the ages of man, upon which the superimposition of white culture was a mere speck in time.

The match, having burnt slowly and smoothly in the windowless room, went out. He lit another and turned around, and there stood the spidery dancer, his blackened skin glistening with sweat, his fierce eyes aglow with the very flames of the match.

One soft cry escaped Reed's lips. But the man made no effort to move, and they stood three feet apart, the intruder and the stranger; beneath the painted white star, those eyes glared unrelentingly, twin orange slits of fire, each a perfect mirror of the match flame.

A long, bony arm rose up from the side; its scaly, tendril-like fingers closed firmly around Reed's throat.

"I prefer the darkness," he hissed, and the match expired.

The heat of his words blasted Reed's face, and in the enveloping darkness, the eyes expanded like a cat's into two bright round pools, no longer reflecting the match but emanating from another source altogether, a place beyond darkness. Moving with their blurry heat, the waving lines of crimson orange light opened into an infinity of their own, where an eternal scourge burned ceaselessly on the fuel of human futility, into which Dylan Reed, still gripped by the throat, looked straight into hell.

"Take a good look," spat the voice into the darkness.

In terror, he lashed out with his fists, like a dreamer caught in a horrible nightmare. His hands sank into flesh, again and again, at first having no effect. Then, with a soft grunt, his throat came free. Ducking, scrambling for balance, he ran helter-skelter through the void, searching desperately for a way out, the hot breath of the spidery man on his heels. He stumbled and fell, rolling onto his back. A leathery hand grabbed his ankle as he looked up and saw the last of the three stars in Orion's belt shining like a beacon from the world above. He was under the opening. Flailing wildly, he found the rope and with both hands lifted his upper body off the dirt, kicking his feet to free himself from the grasping hands of the nether world. With a superhuman effort, he got free and climbed the rope, dragging the other's weight, feverishly trying to leave behind the moaning, aching voices of those souls he heard trapped below.

A second star appeared above, then a third as Dylan Reed fought with his whole being for the right to reenter the world of light; and with each bit of progress, hand over hand, straining and groping, the weight on his feet grew less, until he emerged at the top of the opening and was greeted with the last pailful of cold, wet water, full in his face.

Hands took him by the shoulder; whimpering, drained, he was powerless to resist as they lay him on the ground and rolled him over. Then no one touched him, as he lay in the dirt, gasping for breath, until his presence of mind returned and he rubbed his eyes and could see again. There he lay, looking up at the black hair, sunbaked faces, and midnight eyes of the Indian men, staring in shock at the white face they had just initiated into their most sacred order.

Chapter 16

—◦◦◦—

THEY LED HIM TO A SMALL WHITE HOUSE WITH ONE WHITEWASHED room and left him on a mattress. But no sooner was he asleep than he found himself standing on the plateau above the canyon, where two nights earlier they had made love. This time, however, he was alone. It was raining, and the sky flashed white intervals, followed closely by the boom of thunder. The vast latticework of electric blue streaks, zeet-zeeting to and fro among the clouds and down to the earth, pulsated in the black sky like an out-of-time strobe light, leaving faint trails of smoke in its wake.

Squinting through the storm, Reed sighted the great red insect eye across the canyon just as, with a loud whack, the bolt hit the tower beneath it. Whistling as it raced through the steel veins, the electricity was glowing and shimmering, flaming like a great tree in the distance; the solitary red bulb bulged like a tiny nova staring wide-eyed over its desert domain. Then, with a soft pop, it expired, and the sky danced with streaks of fire in the deep, dark night.

He awoke in the sunlit room, lying on his side. The mattress, barely inches off the floor, was at one end; remaining motionless, in case he was being watched, he squinted through the light of day to see where he was.

A few feet away, a young woman was standing in a metal basin, turned sideways from him, watching herself in a mirror. Thick, blonde hair tied in a yellow bandanna, she rubbed soap over her bare shoulders and breasts; then, lovingly, absorbing the pleasure of it, she squeezed a sponge slowly over herself, letting the water trickle down her body, shivering as she rinsed off. Lingering at each stage of the process, she repeated the soaping and sponging of her fair skin, down the front, then her backside, then down each smooth, slender leg. When she reached the brightly red-painted toenails of each foot, she stood up and examined herself in the mirror, basking in the sun shining through the window glass. With tiny prisms of color forming in the droplets of water sliding down her full breasts, hanging momentarily on her nipples before dropping into space, she stood still for a long time; drying in the warm sunlight, she seemed as enchanted with her reflection as if she were posing for a classic painting. After a while, she toweled herself off, then released the pile of golden hair so that it cascaded halfway down her back. Unsnarling it with her right hand, she admired herself once more in the mirror for a moment, then went to a backpack propped against the wall, took out a pair of white panties and a snug pink tee-shirt, and put them on. Returning to the mirror, she picked up a pair of thick black-rimmed eyeglasses from a nearby shelf and placed them on her nose. Then, still holding it, she set the yellow bandanna by the primitive sink.

Suddenly, she whirled and faced Reed, who lay on his side across the room, his eyes wide open. She opened her mouth to speak, then thought better of it and laughed out loud instead, her face blushing bright red.

"Well," she said finally, a voice light and musical despite her embarrassment. "Was that worth the price of admission?"

"I didn't mean to intrude," he said, not looking at her eyes.

She laughed again, then went to the backpack and pulled out a pair of blue jeans, talking as she put them on.

"My name's Elizabeth. I'm a grad student. And yourself?"

"My name's Reed."

"I didn't know you were there. They didn't tell me anything, just to share this house. Are you studying here, too?"

"Not really. What are you studying?"

Her pale eyes widened through the thick glasses.

"This village. I'm doing my thesis on their family structures, the transfers of land among families and generations, that sort of thing. For my doctoral thesis, in anthropology."

He nodded.

"I'm from Minnesota, the University of Minnesota. Yourself?"

"Back east," he said.

Again her eyes got wide.

"Are you here for healing?"

"For what?"

"For healing. I'm really into healing myself, especially healing the soul. I think we all need to heal our souls of the pain we've taken on."

He sat up, noticing he had fallen asleep with all his own clothes on.

"Well, actually, I'm just passing through," he said, looking at her, smiling.

"Oh," she pouted, taking out a jean jacket. "Well, I'm off to an interview. See you later, maybe. What's your name again?"

"Reed."

"Well, help yourself to coffee and whatever's in the fridge. Bye." And she vanished out the door, letting it bang shut behind her.

Coffee. It had been days since he had had coffee. Back in Chicago, he drank it constantly; it and his typewriter were what writing was about.

He got up, lit the two-burner stove, and filled the sackcloth strainer with ground canned powder; in the time it takes water to boil, Dylan Reed was sitting on a chair, sipping the bitter, wonderful brew. He could have been anywhere; yet here he was, alone in the little white house, in the middle of the desert, drinking coffee.

There was a deck of cards on the table. With a start, he remembered the last time he'd seen cards, in a jail cell with Geller. He picked up the top card and turned it over but barely noticed the deuce of diamonds, his mind drifting back to that other sunlit room.

"You will be able to sense the approach of others—use your breathing," he recalled. As he inhaled sharply, he turned in his chair to find Michael Lanaka standing in the doorway, wearing a red and white checkered shirt and blue jeans.

"I was just about to knock," he said stiffly.

Reed nodded quietly.

"Want some coffee?" he offered at last. Gratefully, Lanaka stepped through the door into the house.

"Thank you. May I sit down?"

"Why ask me?" Reed said, waving at a vacant chair. He drained the thermos into a second cup, pouring the last drops into his own, and handed over the black brew without a word. Silent, they sat staring into their cups, each waiting for the other to speak.

"It's good," Lanaka said at last. "You knew Geller?"

"You might say we were roommates. And yourself?"

"What?"

"How did you know him?"

The black-haired man crossed his legs and took another sip; Reed sat back, watching him squirm, expecting an evasive answer.

"He came here a few years ago looking for knowledge. Doing research, he called it."

"What sort of knowledge?" Reed asked, feigning disinterest. But for once, the Indian wanted to talk.

"He studied our traditions, our beliefs. He said there was a wisdom here that has been lost elsewhere."

Reed stared into the cup in his hands, watching the oily surface drift aimlessly around in the coffee.

"What exactly are your beliefs?" he asked.

Lanaka uncrossed his legs and planted his feet on the floor. He looked like a man about to get up and leave, but he remained seated, holding his cup on his knee.

"Our way is handed down from long ago. We came here, many generations past, after long periods of wandering and hardship. Now we pray to the spirits, live a simple life, take care of the land. We believe we take care of this land for the Creator and He will take care of all the land and us. This is our responsibility. And we seek the blessings of the spirits in the seasons and in our work here."

He paused and looked once around the room; Reed did not interrupt.

"Geller said once, 'In the abstract, this is the truest religion I have encountered.' I think he had seen a great deal of the world. We showed him our spirits, the coyote, the snake, the eagle, and the spider."

As he spoke the last, his opaque eyes came up directly to meet Reed's for the first time. But the younger man kept his quiet.

"Anyway," Lanaka continued slowly, "Geller saw as much of our sacred life as any white man was ever permitted to see. But he was never initiated, as you are. So I must ask: what did Geller teach you?"

Reed sat up slightly.

"What do you mean, initiated?"

"You received, last night, the same as the men of our sacred society. To accept their new status, as fully awakened to our teachings. And yet, you know nothing of these teachings, I think. But you emerged from darkness into light, and you would bathe in our sacred water. It is not something we can undo now. One of our own men, a good man, remained down there, and you emerged in his place. The spirits have acted."

Reed set down his cup, stood up, and went over to the mirror. He studied his own unshaven face, his own shaggy blond hair, and looked at Lanaka's face in the reflection, finding it clearly troubled by this unexpected turn of events.

"Am I supposed to stay here? And who's this girl?" he asked, still keeping his back to the man.

"You will be safe here if you wish to stay."

"And you've arranged for someone to keep me happy. Is that it?"

"We keep this house for those who are not from our own families." The man shrugged. "She is an anthropologist. We have them here all the time."

Reed watched him in the mirror; Lanaka caught on and looked into the glass from his seat, straight into Reed's eyes.

"But what did Geller teach you, Mr. Reed? And what is it that has brought you here like this? What are you running from?"

Reed went back to his chair, sat down, and looked straight into the eyes of the man in the checkered shirt.

"He taught me too much to tell you in a very short time. He asked me to carry on for him somehow, but he died soon after that—so I was told, anyway—and then I escaped."

"Escaped?"

"Yes."

"You are a criminal?"

"Merely a fugitive."

It was Lanaka's turn to squint and study his adversary.

"Did you do it?"

"As I said before, no."

"Why did you run away?"

Reed looked at his feet a moment, thinking.

"It just happened, all at once. I couldn't prove I didn't do it, either, so I didn't go back."

"I see. And now here you are. Well, tell me: What did you learn last night?"

There was the echo of a chill through his entire body.

"Is that your God, that spider? Is that who you pray to?" he asked slowly, his voice dry and weary.

Lanaka winced.

"He is not our God, Mr. Reed. But we are not naive. We seek the truth in whatever manner it speaks to us. The falsest of worlds may have the most beautiful face, but it will surely fall, for that is the way of God. And when his lightning strikes, we asked the spider to spare us, as you say in your 'Lord's Prayer,' deliver us from evil, do you not?"

Reed said nothing.

"We pray for deliverance, then, as you were delivered last night."

The two men lapsed into their separate silences, merging into the stillness of a small house in the desert. Somewhere not too far away, someone was hammering a nail.

"Where's Rosalie?" Reed demanded quietly.

The man in the checkered shirt recoiled visibly, then stood up.

"Tomorrow at sunset, you may go to the spring below the village. There you will find your answer. Now I must ask you not to intrude on us anymore with your surprises. If you wish to learn our ways, please come to the dance on Saturday morning, and we will share them with you."

He paused, standing beside the seated white man.

"I'll think it over," Reed replied without looking up.

"Do not miss your appointment at sunset tomorrow. There will not be another, Mr. Reed."

The thin door banged shut behind him as Reed sat quietly, without moving. He waited until the footsteps had faded, then got up and washed his face and hands in the sink. There were no towels; after wiping his hands on the nearby yellow bandanna, he left the little white house, with its one room and its pretty woman.

⌬

In the night, he woke to hear thunder rolling in the distance. He went to the edge of the cave, but there was no rain; he ascended the handholds and sat on the edge of the cliff, taking in the vast landscape. In the distance, the single red light pulsed intermittently, unperturbed, as over his shoulder, the occasional flash of desert lightning was coming closer, rumbling slowly across the earth.

He stood and began walking, quickening his pace, following the line where the stone cliffs wound their way around the canyon. The first drops of rain pelted him as he jumped across a thin ravine of sand that opened beneath his feet. He was running now, trying to outrace the storm that clearly was gathering force, turning the scene bright with increasing frequency. He cut to his right, tracing a long, thin arc of canyon that ran out with a thirty-foot drop; curling around it, he resumed his way along the cliffs, noting that the spindly tower with its single red eye was a little closer, and, as he tacked back and forth along the rim, straight ahead.

A flash of lightning hit behind him, burning the sparse grass of the high desert, and the thunder was immediate. He ran faster, somehow narrowly avoiding the edge twice, veering away just in time, and after one last, large curve around a dead-end river of sand, he emerged onto a flat plane of dirt and scrub. From here, he could see the feet of the great tower, planted in the dirt; looking up, he was first blinded by rain, until he saw, high in the black sky ahead, the large, solitary red light, blinking monotonously through the tempest.

"Come on," he yelled over his shoulder. "Over here!"

It seemed to Dylan Reed as if the lightning hit right where he'd just been, but he was fifty yards away by then, running toward the steel tower dead ahead. It followed him right across the plain, blasting the dirt with random injections of fire as it sought its elusive target.

"Right here!" he shouted again and again, as if possessed; into the wall of water slamming his face, he ran forward across the open land, zigzagging through the storm as if it were a hail of bullets, trusting in speed and blind luck.

He reached the tower and dove headfirst under its massive legs, as the steel exploded overhead and throbbed with color, turning glistening drops of water into steam. The structure groaned and sagged downward, as if it were going to fall; then, it stopped moving with a loud clank. Lightning hit a distant scrub bush, turning it ablaze, and a moment later, thunder rolled. The storm was moving on.

Reed crawled out from under the steel tower. He had to walk forward twenty steps before he could clearly see the top, where the red light lay dark.

Chapter 17

———⟨𝓥𝓥𝓥⟩———

IN THE LATE AFTERNOON, ELIZABETH PARKER ADMIRED HERSELF in the mirror for a moment before lighting the stove under the kettle. Stripping to a pink tee-shirt and panties, she did some stretching exercises, unaware of the dark eyes watching her through the rear window of the house, studying her smooth, fluid movements. She rubbed her hands once over her body to wake up her circulation in the chilly air.

The kettle came to a whistling boil, and she poured some hot water into the ready sackcloth. There was a knock at the door.

"Come in," she called, quickly pulling on a flannel shirt and wrapping herself in it. Michael Lanaka, wearing a clean blue and white checkered shirt, stood inside the doorway.

"Are you alone?" he asked.

She grinned, waving her hand at the empty room.

"Nobody here but us chickens. Haven't seen him since yesterday."

She poured him a cup of the hot coffee, and then one for herself. She handed his to him and sat down. Lanaka stood quietly for a moment, then took the other chair.

"I wonder where he goes," he mused.

⟨𝓥⟩

It had been a long day of waiting, staying out of sight. Now a single bright light in the evening sky, the unblinking Venus shone above where the last rays of the sun made a thin red line on the western horizon. Crouched behind a small bush, Dylan Reed watched the spring fifty feet away. The minutes went by and, from time to time, he shifted his gaze to the deepening heavens, where stars popped into view as if by magic.

And then she was there, a quiet hooded shape of white cloth, having descended the trail from the village above. Carrying a large jar, the visitor threw off the hood, letting the thick expanse of long hair fall against her white robe and pale face; then, she knelt beside the well.

He wanted to run to her as fast as his legs could carry him, but he moved slowly, silently, breathing more easily now, studying the woman he loved. She knelt there for far longer than it took to fill the large jar she carried, as if this was how she wished him to see her. Then, shrugging under her cloak, she stood up and turned around to leave, to quit their rendezvous, and there he was.

"Reed," she gasped, almost dropping the water pitcher.

"Hold it," he said, trying to smile. "I want to remember you just like you are."

She set down the water and lunged at him from ten feet away, wrapping him in her arms; but when he tried to kiss her, she stepped back.

"Please don't," she said. "They may be watching."

"Then let's get out of here. Come on. What are we waiting for?"

Instead, she sat down on the wooden bench, staring at the ground.

"What you been doing?" she inquired, as if they were old chums meeting by accident.

"Looking for you, mostly," he answered. "Where have you been?"

"I've been all right. Reed, you can stay here now. They told me it's safe, they'll protect you. I know you didn't kill that man, so why don't you just stay here?" He sat down next to her, but she still would not look at him.

"Rosalie, what's going on?" he asked.

"That medallion means something to them; they think you're some kind of lost white brother. *Pahana*, that's the word I heard them use. They say you've already joined the people."

The breeze picked up slightly, murmuring far away in the underbrush. "Who are they, Rosalie? Do you mean Lanaka and that old man?" She nodded without raising her eyes.

"Yes, I knew them when I was here before."

She sat on the bench, her hands folded on her lap, chewing her lip. Softly taking her hand in his, he lowered his voice and spoke gently.

"Rosalie, please look at me."

She moved very slowly, as if afraid. At last, she met his glance with hers, and those beautiful blue eyes he had thought would be with him always were rimmed with moisture.

"Are you going to tell me what's happened?" he persisted in his quiet way.

She pursed her lips.

"You're safe here, Reed. Isn't that what you wanted?"

"I want us to be together, Rosalie. I want to know why you left."

There was a long breath.

"There's something I have to tell you. I …"

She looked away, far away, into the desert, where the last few shapes were fading into the dark.

"What is it?" He slid closer on the bench, his arm around her.

"I have a five-year-old daughter here. Her name is Lisa. And a husband. If I stay with them, you will be safe. Only … we can't see each other," she finished, awaiting the outburst she knew would come.

At first, he stood up as if yanked by an invisible chain; then, with a great effort, he controlled himself, shaking his head, standing there before her.

"I don't know, Reed, everything happened so fast, and we needed somewhere to hide, somewhere no one would expect us to go. I used to live here until I left with Geller. Three years ago. And met you." She looked at him; he stood there, his hands in his pockets, shivering.

"Are you going to say anything?" she said.

"Why didn't you tell me this before?"

"I don't know," she shook her head. "It just never seemed like the right time. And you are always so self-absorbed."

He took a long breath.

"Let me get this straight. You ran off with Geller from here? Leaving a husband and daughter behind?"

"I was his student. Well, his lover too, I guess, but that's not important now. The fact is you are safe. No one will find you here. And Lisa is so pretty, I … I didn't know what it would be like, but now that I have her back, I can't just give her up."

Now she waited as he stared angrily at the dirt.

"Remember how you felt about Timmy?" she prodded. "That made me aware of how much I missed my daughter."

"Yes." He nodded, still dazed. "But I wasn't kissing you off."

"You were heading for Jamaica, as I remember," she answered, ignoring his rebuke.

He paced around the bench, unable to contain himself. But the woman he loved sat impassively, staring at the ground.

"I don't believe this," he said. "I thought you loved me."

She looked up at him, wounded.

"I do love you, Reed. But this is how it is."

"You have another man, too? Just like that. What's his name?"

"John."

"Is he one of these people?"

"These people are very beautiful, and yes, he is." She blinked. "He is one of the tribal policeman."

Reed nodded slowly.

"So, he can guarantee I won't be caught."

"Something like that."

"In return for you."

This time, she said nothing. He waited.

"Well, I …" she began but stopped.

"Tell me," he said. "Does he get all of you?"

She tried to hide her face from him.

"He's very angry that I left, that I disgraced him. So he hasn't made it an issue—sex, that is, if that's what you mean." Then she turned toward him again.

"How's your anthropologist?"

He finally reached the boiling point.

"Is that what they told you?" he confronted her.

"I'm sorry," she said, covering her eyes. "I know it isn't true. Maybe it would be better if it were."

He sat down quickly.

"Rosalie, we can leave here, we can be together. We'll bring Lisa with us if that's what it takes."

But now she stood up and walked a few steps away, standing with her back toward him.

"Reed, tell me something. Where were you really that night?"

"What night?"

"The night that man was killed in Connecticut."

He studied her face, her eyes.

"You think I killed him?"

"No, I didn't say that," she replied quickly, "but I wonder what you think. Why did they arrest you for it?"

He stared at the ground in front of him.

"Whatever else I've done," he said, "I didn't kill that man."

She shifted her weight, watching him, her arms folded across her breast.

"What else have you done?" she asked quietly.

He took a long breath.

"I killed a man once in Vietnam. I stood up in a foxhole, and there he was. Point blank—it was him or me. But I'm no hero. In the war, I just stayed alive. And I blew up a factory once. And I left a woman with my child. But I didn't kill the drug agent. All I did was run away. All my life, that's what I've done, run away."

"So that night, you were fighting in the French and Indian War," she went on.

She saw him slumped forward, mulling it over, trying to answer the unanswerable.

"I don't know," he said finally. "It seemed real at the time." And as if a long-dammed spring inside had suddenly opened, he began to weep, his shaking body doubling over, as he wrapped his arms around his midsection, fat tears raining on the hard-baked desert.

It was growing dark. She waited for him to stop crying as he stared at the ground, refusing to look up at her. But her own breathing had grown harder in tandem with his outburst of pain, and she could not leave him like this. Gingerly she sat down beside him, his back still toward her, and put her hands on his shoulders. He didn't move. Slowly, she rested her face against his back.

"Reed, I do love you," she whispered, "but I have to go now."

He turned and gathered her in his arms, and she buried her face in his chest, soaking his shirt with her own tears, the two lovers crying, unashamed. She began kissing him where his denim shirt was open at the collar, until she had crossed his chin and found his mouth. And for a moment, she gave herself to him, straightened him and pressed herself into his hard, lean body, trying to pour everything into him one last time.

"Oh, Reed," she cried out as she felt herself moving, her mouth now against his forehead, her hands around his neck, "not here."

And then she was pushing herself away from him, pushing him back, so that he stopped and looked at her without saying a word, and let his hands fall to his sides. She slid away, breathing heavily, her face covered with tears. And she turned and ran twenty steps up the trail before he could speak.

"Rosalie," he called, softly.

She stopped, but did not face him.

"Do you believe in magic?" he called to her.

She waited, unsure how to respond. Then she spun toward him, toward the well where he'd come for answers.

"Please, Reed, I have to go now," she began, but the thin breeze blew across her words. No one was there; only the water pitcher remained on the bench. She took a deep breath and went back, twenty steps down the path, and picked up the jar, holding it to her chest with both arms. Then, once again, she began the long climb up the trail, crying softly to herself.

Chapter 18

——◦◦◦——

"HAVE YOU TOLD HER YET?"
The question, out of the blue, startled the man lying flat on the hard mattress. He looked up at the stunning blue eyes of the woman above him, but just as quickly, he looked away, preferring to respond by driving further into her so that she could do nothing but feel the intense pleasure of their loving. She sat up straight, closed her eyes, and put her hands behind her head, arching herself up and backward; as they rose together to the heights, his large hands enjoyed all of her, caressing her legs and back side, palming her smooth, firm breasts, grasping her shoulders beneath the flowing blonde hair. At last, they finished together, collapsing into a long, passionate kiss, their bodies throbbing with waves of release. She took her mouth off his and moaned loudly, then buried it into the curve of his neck.

They lay like this for several minutes, until their breathing returned to normal. Elizabeth Parker sat upright again and smiled. She ran her hand across the smooth, russet-colored chest of the black-haired man, looked into his dark eyes, and found him, as always, the handsomest man she had ever loved.

"Have you told her yet?" she whispered.

The man realized he could no longer ignore the question.

"Who?" he answered noncommittally.

"Your wife."

"Told her what?"

"About us, John," she answered.

The man sat up and took her breast with his mouth, running his tongue over the small red center.

"Oh, John," she said through her heavy breath, "you are still in love with her, aren't you?" She pushed him away, gently but firmly, back onto the mattress.

"I don't even know her anymore," he said with a shrug.

"Do you want to?" She searched the opaque black eyes for the truth. But John looked at the watch on his left wrist.

"I've got to pick up my daughter," he said, easing the woman off of him, her long blonde hair wild around her face. He stood up quickly and reached for his clothes. Outside the window, it was getting dark.

"What do you want me to do?" Elizabeth asked quietly as he dressed.

"For now, nothing." He shrugged. "I've got to go." And with a quick kiss on the lips, he was out the door.

❧

Step by step, Rosalie ascended the slim trail. The moon popped in and out of view as she switched back and forth against the side of the rock. Was it rising later, losing its recent fullness? On the way to somewhere else, she saw it thirty-two times, counting each one before she reached the top, and even then, she wished the trip were longer.

Inside the house, her daughter and husband were playing cards on the floor. Lisa opened her mouth in a large grin and held up her cards, shaking her shiny black hair like the little girl she was.

"Mommy, look!" she squealed, but she was quickly scooped up by her father, a tall, broad-shouldered man in the blue uniform of his profession, the tribal police, recognized by the Bureau of Indian Affairs. With his burnt complexion, black hair, and opaque black eyes, he was the mirror image of the little girl in his arms as they disappeared into a dimly lit side room.

"Okay, off to bed," he said.

Rosalie took off her coat and walked back to the front door, staring through the glass at the moon and the black sky. She shook her head to free her long red hair and caught her own eyes in the reflection on the door. A pair of hands touched her gently, at first, then firmly at the waist, and the moon was there again.

"John, please."

He removed his hands and stepped back, but she didn't turn around. Instead, she stood watching the bean-shaped disc of white-yellow rock, hanging in the blackness as if by magic.

He sat on a stuffed chair and watched her. Hands in her pockets, lost in thought, she tried to outwait.

"You wish you were out there," he said dismissively. "Why don't you go?" When she didn't turn around, he lit a cigarette with a chrome lighter, exhaling into the room

She felt a shiver.

"Where?" She knew what he had meant, he knew, and she knew that he knew it. But what could be served by pursuing it?

He sighed resignedly.

"Why don't you come and sit down," he said, waving his hand at the cloth couch across from his chair.

But she said nothing in reply, her thoughts drifting out over the landscape; she felt the breath of the cactus, the small brush, the tall grasses, the sand, the canyon stone, and the open air sweep over her like a steady desert breeze. Running, she would be running now, dashing through the small pines, the ridges left by spring water running off the mesa, running through the glowing white-tinged shapes of the moonlit earth, wild, free, untamed, hungry and cunning like the coyote, the trickster, the spirit of hard-earned lessons.

But her reverie was short-lived.

"I won't hurt you," continued her husband.

⌇

The shapes and colors of Rosalie's dreamscape were, conversely, the actual surroundings through which Dylan Reed, lost in thought,

wandered his way back. As he crossed the public campground, uninhabited in the chilly fall, he felt the presence of others nearby; ducking
behind a small pine tree, he waited as three young Indian men passed,
speaking softly in their own language. They stopped at the pump and
drank a round of water in their cupped hands. When at last they moved
on, Reed continued on through the sandy mesa, his shadow stretching
ever longer before him. It vanished as he reached the edge of the canyon;
he found the handholds and went down into the cave.

Things had been moved. Like an animal sensing a threat, his awareness kicked into overdrive, and he became still. There was no sound of
movement in the night air. No lingering smell. No light but starlight,
no breeze. But his food was gone.

He stood silent in the cover of the cave's darkness, eyeing the vacant night, the moonlit white sandstone bordering the yawning chasm
of blackness where the spring, so tiny at its back, had carved its way
through the ages out to the open desert. And when, having convinced
himself no one was around, and was breathing in a relaxed way, he let
his own thoughts drift into the night.

He had come on the run, to a place where she had said they could
stop running. And now here they were, safe, as long as they remained
apart.

A bird flew into the canyon from behind the rim, soaring downward
into the abyss of sand and rock with a loud screech.

She had left here with Geller and come back with him. It was, for
her, a full circle, he imagined; she had returned to the spot she had left
from. But the thought of her with another man angered him; he saw
her in the arms of the faceless man, yielding herself in a way Reed had
thought she could only have with him. Or would she? How would he
know? She had a husband. And she chose to return to him tonight. She
would be home by now.

As for Dylan Reed, he knew that, for the moment, he was not a
hunted man. And he could stay around this village alone, or he could
go on running somewhere else.

As if the night itself were changing, the slowly drifting shapes and shadows carved by the moonlight began to make sense; he saw, clearly, his situation. He had no food, no money, no means of support, and no shelter for the winter unless he moved into town and accepted their hospitality. Or he could move on. Would she go with him? If they took the little girl, they would be hunted everywhere.

On the ground, the empty canteen lay open, its cap half-buried in the dirt. He would have to walk back to the pump and risk being seen. But instead, he walked out of the cave and into the moonlight, to where it was a six-foot jump down to the first deep creases of sand. Down he went, over small hills of loose dirt, around columns of white and red stone, down along the slender damp impressions left by the fine spring water that, however slight, always seeks the deeper sea.

But what had looked so deceptively simple was, in fact, slow going. He arrived, sweating, breathing hard, at a small ledge, and, looking out, discovered all his labors had brought him only a fraction of the way down. Above, in the distance, was the ever-vigilant red beacon, still blinking mindlessly over the canyon. Now he knew: he wanted to get to where it could not see him.

He caught his breath and continued down, scrambling across one dune, damp with the night air, disregarding it, leapfrogging small stones, picking up speed, slipping, regaining his balance, skimming over the lunar-like surface as if gravity itself need not apply. Feeling like an animal at home on its turf, he eased himself quickly along, down, down the bed of the nearly invisible stream, until he could see ahead the flat, pebbled spot where the canyon bottomed out.

His sneakers filling with loose sand, he let his accelerating pace carry him over the last few ridges of dirt and aimed for the flat basin with reckless abandon, gleefully landing too fast to see until too late that it was merely a ledge, with a ten-foot drop beyond. Unable to stop in time, he flew over the sheet of gray blackstone, changing direction barely enough to land unceremoniously in a large heap of soft sand just a few feet from where the remnants of the forgotten stream dove forever into the earth.

Unhurt but shaken, he pulled himself out of the dune. He emptied his sneakers and caught his breath again, then set out down the wash

created by the annual runoff of spring rain. Now bone dry, it was nothing like the river of his dreams; yet, he knew it, knew its way, its curves,
and he followed it around each bend with his senses alive to the harsh,
pitiless world around him.

There was a quick pain in his midsection; abruptly, he stopped, his
eyes alert at once to the spot where the riverbed wound behind a hill
of red dirt. But he heard nothing; slowly inching his way through the
curve, he saw a flash of white, stepped back quickly, then eased around
the bend once more into an area where the moon shone, unobstructed,
like a shaft of light from above into the deep recess. And there, a few
yards away, two side-by-side holes of darkness sat peering at him like
eye sockets in a pale mask, a face glowing bone white on the sand as if
the rest of the body was buried beneath. He bent over and picked it up,
examining the dry, porous pelvis of some medium-sized animal that
had followed its thirst to a watering hole it had never reached. Now, the
strange rectangular thing with the empty leg joints, open sockets and
handle-like sides were all that remained of its journey.

A bird flew near, mocking him with a loud screech. Whirling, he
put the bone over his face and watched the bird soar away through the
vacant sockets as if through a camera or binoculars. And when the
bird had gone, he surveyed the entire landscape through his new lens,
entranced, until in his wonder he forgot he was wearing it. The giant
parfait of sand and stone, the wasteland that surrounded him, became
alive once more.

Chapter 19

———⟨୭⟩⟨୭⟩———

TWO MEN RODE SILENTLY THROUGH THE EARLY MORNING MIST, OVER the swells and gullies through which the slim ribbon of blacktop wound its way across the desert.

"Twelve hours since the call," one said. "Think he'll still be there?"

They had taken the night flight to Phoenix, sleeping fitfully in the narrow seats, changing planes to get within driving distance of the reservation by morning. They were tired, still wearing the rumpled dark suits, and facing a long day before they would get to sleep.

"I don't know. But we have to start somewhere," the driver replied.

"Where do we meet our contact?"

William Scanlon looked quietly at the other man, reflecting that, no matter how many times he had heard it, the deep, resonant quality of the voice always took him by surprise, as if he were hearing a long-familiar sound.

"At a dance in the main village," he said. "Thanks for coming along." He didn't add they could both be reprimanded for it. But it was a Saturday, a day off, and they had charged the flights to their own credit cards.

"Hey, think nothing of it," said Bob Lake.

⟨୭⟩

As if it were approaching across the sunbaked desert, the wavy figure gradually became more defined, more human, as it stopped twice on its left foot, then twice on its right, its arms extended, circling in place as it gathered into itself the direct sunlight in which it stood. Lying on his side, half-asleep and half-awake, Dylan Reed studied the shimmering form until, suddenly, he knew he was watching himself.

He felt himself howl, a low moan from somewhere deep inside, a sound that became a baby's cried to his ears. Tears flowing, his sobbing grew older, deeper, aging until it had spent itself. Through it all, the glowing dancer continued stepping back and forth, circling, the hands planing the air like wings until, at last, he had no more water, no more sorrow. The sunlit figure began to warm him, to give him its own heat, even as it faded slowly away. And then he was awake, cleansed to the marrow of his being, as he lay there in a deep mood of peace.

The sun eased over the canyon rim and hit his face. He got up immediately and began to act out the dance, stepping twice on each foot, circling, extending his hands and arms. He danced in the sunlight for some minutes before his hands, from habit, tried to rub his eyes. But he was still wearing the white bone mask, tied with a yellow bandanna he had found in his back pocket.

He took it off and laid it gently on the ground. He rubbed his hands together, then his face and eyes, until he felt fully awakened. Then he reached down, picked up the mask, and put it back over his face. He looked out through the eyeholes at the forbidding parfait of sand and stone, the canyon in which he had slept, and smiled. It was alive. He could feel it.

✐

It was a sunny, clear day, and the drums had already begun their steady, rhythmic pounding as the village filled with spectators. Indians from the surrounding towns, whites from the cities with cameras and umbrellas for protection against the sun, all crowded around the main plaza on folding chairs and makeshift benches. A few climbed onto the rooftops, from which they could watch the dance against a backdrop of miles and miles of desert, stretching out far beyond the great rock to where the distant, hazy mountains merged with the blue sky.

A brown and white eagle, chained to a rooftop perch, angrily adjusted its stance with a quiet fluttering of its wings, as the dancers, twenty-two men, emerged from the underground kiva into the light of day. Weaving down the narrow path in single file, each wearing a tall vertical wooden mask topped with different colored feathers, they were otherwise naked above the waist, their skins decorated in streaks of lightning-shaped paint, pointing downward to a skirt of spruce boughs at the midsection, tied in place with a bright sash of red, or blue, or violet, or golden, or green. Below the skirt, each wore rawhide lacing around the lower legs above crude sandals.

In dramatic contrast to the elaborately costumed dancers, the priest directing them wore only a loincloth and a single feather in his hair. Every so often, he called out as each dancer moved in perfect time with the others, slowing down and speeding up together, turning about-face, spinning forward again. At last, the procession reached the main open area, lined up in single formation, and at a signal from the priest, the drumming and dancers stopped as one.

The men broke ranks and began picking up melons, squashes, and ears of corn that had been placed in bundles in the street. These they gave to the older women of the town; then, they returned to their places and began again, stamping a right-footed dance, the left foot never moving. The priest called out, the dancers spun and faced the other way. They stamped thirteen beats, then stopped.

Two women came out and sat down before a small house; one had a skin drum, the other a hard gourd and stick. Grinding and tapping, they set the pace for another dance, in which the drums and the dancers would slow down at various intervals, as if at random—fifteen, twenty-seven, six, seventeen beats apart—and then resume the original tempo just as quickly. In tune with the rhythm and with each other, they continued stamping the right foot, keeping the left one planted, occasionally spinning around to face the opposite direction. Eleven beats after one turn, the priest began to speak to the crowd above the dance in a quavery, lilting voice.

"In the beginning was endless space." He raised his voice. "This was the first world, a world where the Creator lived in peace and beauty. And he created life, plants, animals, stones, and man, and the first people were pure and happy. And this was the second world.

"But soon, the people grew wicked and wanted more than they had, though they had everything. And many forgot the song of the Creator, and those who did sing were laughed at. And there came among them talkers and wicked men who hardened the hearts of the people.

"And so the Creator came to the few who sang to him and said, 'Come.' And they followed many days, until they came to the place where the ant people lived. There they went under the ground, for the Creator was set on destroying the wickedness of the world.

"And the Creator freed the twins who hold the poles of the earth, and they left their places, and the earth began spinning, and the mountains and seas flew at each other, and everything was destroyed that was not with the ants. And when this was done, he reordered the world and drew off the top of the ant kiva, and the people made their emergence to the third world.

"And the third world was a fine and beautiful one, a red world of great richness. And some of the people sang the praises of the Creator from the mountains, but many forgot, and the people built great cities and great machines, with which they attacked each other.

"And so the Creator led the people who sing to the end of the earth, where they found tall plants with hollow stems. 'Cut these and breathe,' he said, 'for I will destroy this world.' And they did this. And a great flood drowned the mountains and broke the continents until they sank. Then the people came forth and sailed many, many days, until they crossed many islands; but each time, they knew this was not the place of their emergence. Until, finally, they found a great land and sailed north and south until they came safely between the great walls of mountains.

"'Here is our place of the emergence,' they shouted with joy, and the Creator appeared before them.

"'Behold the islands you've crossed,' He said, and He sank them all. 'See how I have washed away your footprints. Your proud cities, your earthly treasures are at the bottom of the seas. But the time will come, if you preserve the right way, when these stepping stones will appear to prove the truth you speak.'"

The old priest paused momentarily, noting the brown Bureau of Indian Affairs station wagon that had pulled to a stop at the far end of the street. The drums and scratching gourds still carrying the dancers with their incessant pulse, he watched a large red-skinned man in a blue uniform get out. The priest picked up the rhythm, raised his voice, and began again.

"'This is your new land,' He said. 'The world complete. It is green and barren, warm and cold. Now go, and follow your stars, and you will find your true home. But do not forget the song, for I will listen for you on the tops of the mountains.' And He left them to begin life again in this, the fourth world."

The policeman threaded his way through the crowd to where a red-haired woman in a long white dress was seated on a bench. Aware that many eyes were on them, he took her hand and placed it on his lap. But he did not look at her, for he was searching the crowd for something else. And, at last, he found what he was looking for: two dark-suited men in sunglasses, sitting on a roof ledge from where they could see over the heads of the other spectators.

"Today we announce," the priest continued, "that these young men have survived the third world of chaos. These men before you have emerged from darkness into the fourth world to dance in the light of the sun. And we ask that, with these gifts and this dance, the spirits bless them and welcome them that they may serve the people well through this year and the years to come."

And with that, the music stopped.

The crowd erupted with applause. The dancers stood smiling as several young women rushed out and kissed their young men. The crowd laughed good-naturedly as one large older woman kissed her son. But the dancers stayed in their places, for the day's festivities were just beginning.

John had been at her side for barely a minute when Rosalie felt his hand slip out of hers. She turned and saw a young blonde woman sit down on his other side. The girl was wearing a heavy flannel shirt and thick black-rimmed glasses but was unmistakably good-looking, with a big smile and a sweet face. Pretending to look out over the crowd, Rosalie watched from the corner of her eye as Elizabeth Parker spoke softly into John's ear. He nodded and turned his head to whisper back into hers, and with a flash of insight, Rosalie Lenoir understood why her husband, the father of their daughter, had not insisted on making love. And in this realization, that the hold of desire she had thought to have over him did not, in fact, exist, she knew there was danger.

She looked to her left, and saw that Michael Lanaka was trying to catch her eye across the crowd. He was seated next to the old blind man opposite the priest; as his eyes met hers they directed her up, across the street to the rooftop. Next to the chained eagle, two men in sunglasses were staring straight at her. But when they realized she had seen them, they looked quickly away.

"It's her," she read on the lips of William Scanlon.

The priest clapped his hands once, and everyone cleared the street except for the costumed men. But before he could begin again, there was a collective gasp from the dancers that caused him to stop and turn around. Twenty yards away, a white man stood in the street with his hands in the pockets of his jeans. No one had seen him approach, yet there he stood, in the bright sunlight like some glowing apparition, shirtless, his shaggy blond hair tied back under a yellow bandanna. On his face was a white pelvic bone, upside down, with eyeholes where there had once been leg joints, through which he peered out at the spectacle before him. And as the entire crowd stared back, there was, for the first time, a confused silence in the town.

"Go back where you came from, you kook," yelled a white woman from the gallery. Instead, the man stepped quickly forward, and as a small stone medallion bounced on his chest, the villagers knew this was indeed the man they had heard about.

He stopped before the priest, who studied the mask and eyes.

"So. You have come." The old man spoke quietly. "What is it you want?"

"I was invited," answered Dylan Reed.

The priest looked to his left, to where the blind man sat next to Michael Lanaka. As if he could see everything, the old one nodded and placed his hand on his breast.

"With the others," the priest said, stepping aside and making a downward chop with his hand, like an orchestra conductor. At once, the sound of pulsating drums and grinding wires filled the air, as Reed walked past him and took a place at the end of the long single file of dancers.

Some of the spectators, thinking it was part of the show, clapped their hands together to applaud. But the villagers, aware something extraordinary was occurring, leaned quietly forward to watch the strange white man with the medallion swinging on his chest. At first, he seemed out of step, unable to follow the simple right-footed stamping. Soon, however, they saw he was doing something else entirely, stepping two beats with his right foot, then two with his left, bobbing back and forth until the instruments and dancers all slowed together, everyone spun around, and he was at the front of the procession, spreading his hands out, palms down, as if he were gliding through the air.

One by one, the other dancers began to lose the rhythm as they watched him. The music continued on, and the priest made no sound, as the dancer next to Reed found the beat again, but with his left foot. After two taps he switched to his right, then back to his left, and the man next in line changed also. The new pattern spread contagiously, as all the dancers' left feet alternated with the right, until the sound of the stamping feet became unified with the drums. The priest yelled out, the instruments slowed, and all the dancers spun in place as one, swooping through a quick circle with their hands and arms extended like the wings of an eagle.

The drums picked up speed again, and the new dance continued for some minutes more, the feet alternating, the circling in place, until the stamping, the pounding drums, and the grinding gourds reached a crescendo, arriving at a plateau of intensity that settled over the crowd like a deep peace, a shared awareness that brought a profound quietude. One by one, the spectators sat back and relaxed, mesmerized by the scene before them.

As Reed felt the beat begin to change, he stopped abruptly, and with his last step, the music and the other men's feet finished.

There was a silence of the town, quiet enough to hear the hard breathing of the dancers, as they stood motionless in the sunlit dirt street.

Chapter 20

———◊◊◊———

Dylan Reed looked up and to his right, saw two white men in business suits, ties, and sunglasses, and knew the moment that had been stalking him had arrived. Still slightly out of breath, he watched as the agent he had seen before drew back his jacket to reveal a small black pistol at his belt.

And just as quickly, Michael Lanaka was standing over them.

"Who are you? What do you want?" he demanded.

"FBI. This man is a fugitive, and we're taking him in," replied William Scanlon, nodding at the dance toward the man with the mask on his face.

"Do you have a court order?"

Scanlon looked at his partner. They were there unofficially, but they were there to make an arrest.

"Don't make trouble, or it will rain on you," Bob Lake said portentously.

Lanaka shook his head.

"If you have no court order you must speak with the Grandfather. You are in his jurisdiction."

Lake eyed the small bronzed man in the clean checkered shirt, the black eyes flecked with blue around the edges.

"Listen, Little Big Man, we're taking him out of here one way or the other. And the woman too," he finished, nodding at Rosalie, who was watching this conversation from across the street.

"You must seek the judgment of the Grandfather," Lanaka reiterated. "Come."

The drums began their rhythmic pounding again as the three men stood there. Scanlon, aware he was losing control of the situation, shrugged and adjusted his sunglasses. They stood up.

"Okay," he said. "But no tricks. And they don't leave."

Lanaka signaled separately to Reed and to Rosalie, directing each to a gap in the adobe surrounding the plaza. As the next dance began, they slid through the crowd to the narrow alleyway between the squat mud houses packed together in the town. They arrived at an old door of cardboard and glass that led into a room where the afternoon sun highlighted the dust particles hanging in the air. There were several wooden benches strewn around and one stuffed armchair.

"Wait here," said Michael Lanaka. "I will bring the Grandfather after the next dance."

Bob Lake settled into the stuffed chair with a heavy sigh, sending a wad of dust particles into the sun-streaked air. Dylan Reed sank down to the floor and rested his back against the stucco wall as Scanlon perched on a bench. Only Rosalie remained on her feet, her back to the others, listening to the drums outside.

Reed took off the mask and set it next to him on the floor as William Scanlon began talking.

"Okay, this is how it is. Consider yourselves under arrest as of now, no matter what this man says. You have the right to remain silent. If you choose to give up this right, anything you say can and will be used against you in a court of law. You have the right to an attorney. If you do not have an attorney, one will be appointed to represent you. Do you understand these rights?"

"I'm the attorney for Dylan Reed," Rosalie said, still keeping her back to the room.

"Lady, you are in this too deep," Scanlon said. "You need an attorney yourself."

"Do you have a court order?" she asked. "What exactly is the basis for this arrest?" Scanlon heaved a heavy sigh saved up from the long night and day of travel.

"For him? Murder, conspiracy to distribute contraband, and interstate flight. Not to mention speeding, resisting arrest, and destruction of government property."

"And myself?"

"Accessory to conspiracy, interstate flight, and harboring a fugitive. Is that enough for now?"

She turned and faced the two agents slumped in their seats.

"Whatever you say. But you'll need a court order, or the Grandfather's permission, to take us off the reservation."

"We'll see about that," Lake added.

Outside, the drums continued to throb their steady beat, slowing, speeding up, droning through the dusty town. Scanlon stood up abruptly.

"I'm going out to find the chief," he said.

"Good idea, Bill," answered Lake. "I'll hold the fort." He took off his sunglasses and rubbed his eyes. Rosalie turned back toward the window as Lake looked over to where Reed sat quietly on the floor.

"You know," he began, "there's a way you could make this easy on yourself." His voice, deep and resonant with the persuasiveness perfected in his years as a federal interrogator, made the drums outside fade into the background in the otherwise still room. But Reed said nothing. Undaunted, the agent pressed on.

"You could tell me what you did with the other suitcase," he continued. "It will go easier for you if you cooperate."

Reed squinted at his questioner, watching as he wiped his glasses on his tie; the deep voice implied the seriousness of his question.

"What other suitcase?" he said at last.

"Sure, sure, play it cool," Lake replied, keeping his tone confidential and friendly. "Okay, let's try again. The suitcase with the real goods. Where is it? You help us, we may be able to help you, 'cause take my advice, you're going nowhere fighting this thing."

But Reed furrowed his brow, puzzled.

"I don't know what you're talking about," he said.

Lake took out a pack of cigarettes and tapped one free as he spoke.

"Of course you do. And if you want to play ball, you're going to have to be realistic."

The door opened just as Rosalie spun around and took a hard look at Bob Lake, stretched out on the armchair with a cigarette dangling in his fingers. Scanlon entered the house, followed by John and Elizabeth Parker.

"The old man is coming right after this dance," Scanlon said. "And here's the local assistance."

Rosalie faced her husband across the room.

"So it was you," she said as if she had already known.

"It's my job." He shrugged and turned away.

"All right, all right," Lake cut in. "Enough of that. Everybody, grab a seat so we get this worked out."

"I'm going back out for a minute," Scanlon said.

"Sure thing," Lake agreed. "Everything's just fine here." Scanlon left again, and the room grew quiet. The sound of drums seeped into every crack in the old house, as if the straw fibers vibrated inside the hard-baked mud blocks of the walls. Lake lit another cigarette and watched the smoke move through the sunlight.

"Come on. It won't do you any good to hold out," he said to Reed. But the man on the floor picked up the white bone mask and ran his finger slowly around the edge of the eye sockets, and had no response. Finally, Elizabeth Parker could stand it no longer.

"Has anybody ever told you," she gushed to Bob Lake, "you sound just like Elvis?"

Lake grinned at her.

"Lady, as far as you're concerned, I am Elvis," he said, purposely exaggerating his voice to enhance the effect. "Ah mean, that's what they say."

Rosalie turned to face him.

"What else do they say, Mr. Lake?" she asked nastily.

"Hey, take it easy, lady," he shot back. "You'd be better off getting your boyfriend here to get smart," and he blew a smoke ring through his rounded lips.

"That's right, Mr. Lake, we've all got to be realistic," she said quietly.

"That's what I always say." He smiled at her.

"Listen," John said. "The drums have stopped." They sat quietly for a minute, wondering if the drumming would begin again. But soon, they could hear the voices and footsteps of the tourists leaving the village, filing through the narrow alleys toward the cars parked out by the highway. At last, the door opened, and Scanlon, Lanaka, and the old blind man walked in; the ancient one went directly to the stuffed chair, and Lake barely escaped before he sat down on him.

"What is it you wish to ask?" Lanaka began.

William Scanlon sat down on a wooden bench and placed his hands on his knees. He had removed his sunglasses and looked very tired around the eyes.

"We represent the United States government, which has declared these two fugitives from justice. We are arresting them and taking them into custody for trial."

"You are aware," Lanaka answered, "you have no jurisdiction on this reservation? And no court order? Why do you have no court order if it is as you say?"

"Your jurisdiction is for your people and does not cover escaped criminals avoiding the laws of the United States," the agent replied.

Lanaka translated this conversation as the old man rocked slowly on his chair, his hands folded on his lap. When the blind man spoke, Lanaka looked at him sharply, as if he had said something strange; they had a brief exchange, until Scanlon interrupted.

"What is he saying?"

"He says there will be rain. Much rain."

Lake stood up from the bench.

"Hey, that's great, just like in the movies. Listen, I don't doubt you can use some rain around here, but we'll be long gone by then."

The old man made a chopping motion with his hand and spoke a quick flurry of ancient words.

"He says, as you are men of violence, you will bring this rain on yourselves," Lanaka continued. "He says you are very wrong. I'm not sure exactly what he means."

"Yeah, well, listen, it's time to go," Lake declared.

"I know what he means," Rosalie interjected, turning away from the window.

Everyone stopped to look at her once, standing there in the long white dress, pushing her wild, untied hair from her face.

"Mr. Lake," she began, "didn't I hear you ask Mr. Reed about the suitcase with the real goods?"

Lake shifted his weight.

"Just trying to find out the facts," he replied.

But she pressed on.

"Isn't it true, Mr. Scanlon, that the suitcase you found in Florida had nothing in it but sand and old clothes?"

Scanlon ran a hand through his thinning hair.

"Yes, that's correct. Why?"

"There was another suitcase of sorts, or at least another suitcase worth of goods, Mr. Scanlon. I emptied the contents myself, the 'real goods,' as you call them, into the ocean, and filled it up with sand and old clothes before he delivered it."

The old man of the stuffed chair was vigorously nodding his head.

"I still don't see where this is going, Miss Lenoir," Scanlon said.

"All the time we were on the boat, the men kept dropping their voices down low and saying, 'Well, boys, we gotta be realistic,'" she said, dropping her voice down.

"Now I know why. They were imitating you," she finished, addressing Bob Lake, who was putting his sunglasses back on.

Lake sighed heavily.

"I don't know what you're trying to do here, lady, but it's time to get moving," Lake said. He went over to Reed and stood above the seated suspect, still leaning against the wall.

"On your feet," he ordered.

But Rosalie stepped between them.

"Forgive me, Reed," she said quietly. "I never really knew for sure until now that you had nothing to do with this all along." She turned toward Scanlon, who had not moved.

"What you should know, Mr. Scanlon, is that I never told anyone about switching the contents of the suitcase. Not even Reed." Continuing on, she circled the room once, working it out in her head.

"In fact, there's no way anyone could know there ever were real goods in the suitcase to begin with," she went on, spiraling through the smoke clouds hanging in the sun-streaked room.

"Unless, that is," she said, arriving face to face in front of Bob Lake, "he was there to pack it himself."

The old blind man nodded and relaxed deep into his chair.

"Nice try, Miss Lenoir, but it doesn't work," Lake said, shaking his head. "Let's go, Bill." But she stepped a foot closer, practically nose to nose with him.

"Did you kill Giles, too?" she asked softly.

Like matching poles of a magnet, they were too close together to stay where they were; it was Lake who stepped nervously backward, seeing everyone in his peripheral vision.

"Don't try to confuse things, lady. Bill, let's get the show on the road."

William Scanlon seemed genuinely taken aback.

"How did you know about the other suitcase, Bob?"

"There is no other suitcase."

"But you said there was."

"I'm just trying to get them to open up. You're not buying into this, are you?" Lake regarded his partner, his deep voice rising ever so slightly. "It was in all the reports. Everybody knew."

"Is that true, Mr. Scanlon? Did you know there was a second suitcase?" Rosalie asked.

Scanlon scratched his head and stared across the small room at his partner.

"No, I didn't," he answered very slowly.

The room suddenly darkened as the bright daylight outside was overtaken by clouds roaming the vast desert plain. The old man spoke quickly.

"What did he say?" Scanlon asked, distracted.

Lanaka sat down on a bench.

"He says the rain has come."

Scanlon nodded as if this remark made the most sense of anything he had heard recently.

"I've been wondering why you have such an interest in this case, Bob," he said at last.

"I'm a team player. And I told you, Giles was my friend, too."

Agent Scanlon nodded again as he thought it over, and for a moment, he seemed to be accepting this explanation, until his bobbing head began moving from side to side instead, and he frowned.

"You know, Bob, I risked a lot coming here today. And so did you. Too much for Giles' sake. Or for me. You are too … realistic."

Lake studied the face of his partner.

"What are you saying?"

"I think when we get back, we'll have to check this out further. Ask some questions. You know, do an investigation."

There are moments in the desert when the wind rises up and seeps through closed doors and windows, through the walls of houses, even through the middle of a conversation. And as the oncoming storm outside sent a wind between the two federal agents, there was a dead silence. Bob Lake looked into the eyes of his partner, the man he had come across the country with, to avenge the death of their friend and fellow agent, and did not like what he saw.

With a rapid motion, he reached inside his jacket and drew out a small, black pistol.

"All right," he said. "Enough is enough."

Chapter 21

—⦿—

WITH THE GUN BARREL POINTED AT HIS FACE, WILLIAM SCANLON understood at last.

"So, Bob, did you kill Giles, too?" he asked quietly.

Bob Lake shifted the weight on his feet, mulling over just how much he wanted to say.

"What happened to Giles was he got greedy. Now, Bill, give me your gun. Carefully."

Scanlon reached into his waistband and drew out his weapon, extending it to Lake.

"Where are you going to go, Bob? Why don't you let us work this out?"

Lake snorted a quick laugh and stuck the pistol in his belt.

"Always the good cop," he answered. His tired, unshaven face tightening with resolve, he sorted through his prospects.

"You," he waved the gun at John, "you can drive us out of here. On your feet. And you're coming, too," he finished, grabbing Rosalie's arm and digging the gun into her ribs.

"The rest of you, on the floor with the bonehead over there," he jerked his head in Reed's direction, the deep voice decidedly edgy. Everyone obeyed except the Grandfather, who remained quietly motionless as Scanlon, Lanaka, and Elizabeth Parker sat gingerly on the floor next to Reed, who had not moved or spoken the entire time.

"Now everybody knows what to do, right? Absolutely nothing. That way, no one will get hurt. Do you understand?"

"You'll never get away with this," said federal agent Scanlon.

"Yeah, that's what I always heard. Well, this job paid shit anyway," Bob Lake replied.

The outside world barely noticed as the three of them, John, Rosalie, and Bob Lake, filed through the narrow dirt alleyways toward the brown station wagon parked at the edge of the plaza. It was about a hundred yards to the car, and Lake, the gun ready inside his pocket, looked straight ahead, paying no attention to the villagers milling in the streets, celebrating their festival in the aftermath of the tourist invasion. The sky was rapidly darkening, and a light rain had begun falling as they threaded their way.

"What do you need me for?" Rosalie asked quietly. "You can travel faster without me."

But Bob Lake gripped her arm tightly and grunted a low laugh.

"Come on, honey, you don't seriously think I buy that bit? You want to live, you're coming with me," he answered.

"You're wrong. There's nothing for me to show you."

"Yeah, sure, keep it up."

By the time they reached the car, the rain had picked up and was falling steadily, fat pellets of water turning the street into a thin layer of mud. Only John and Rosalie knew that in seconds, the rain could turn the dirt streets of the town into unmanageable slop, but they said nothing as Lake directed John to drive and pushed Rosalie into the backseat, sliding next to her with the gun ready in his hand. Already the rain was pounding hard on the roof of the car.

Inside the house, the deep voice of Bob Lake still hung heavy in the dusty air. Quickly Reed stood up.

"Where are you going?" Scanlon demanded as he too got to his feet.

"Fuck you," he replied, and he rushed out the door.

The Indian men and women who had paid little attention to Lake and his party were still standing around as they emerged into the street. A young man who'd danced with him came over to offer his hand, but Reed slapped his palm and kept moving.

"Come on," he said, breaking into a run. As if an hourglass had been turned and all the grains of sand were flowing toward the opening, the villagers began to follow Reed, pouring through the dirt streets toward the point at which the only principal street on the island mesa converged onto the narrow strip of land that led out to the highway.

At the other end of town, John eased the car into gear and weaved slowly through the rutted dirt, winding his way between the mud houses as the rain increased. On the far side of these houses, built countless generations before, the sheer walls of the cliffs dropped hundreds of feet to the desert below. They approached the last houses; from here, it was a flat dirt road to the highway with one turn and two hundred yards of rocks and mud, and a drop of five hundred feet on each side. John turned on the headlights and wipers as the rain splattered the windshield with increasing fury.

"Step on it," Lake ordered. John pressed the accelerator, and the brown station wagon fishtailed across the road, sliding through a turn with the deep desert looming directly in front of the windshield.

"This is too fast!" John shouted, as he fought to control the car, squinting through the rain, the wet street becoming a brown soup before his eyes. He looked out over the cliffs as they rounded the last corner, clearing the final houses before the last stretch to the highway, a narrow strip of increasingly treacherous mud.

But there was a crowd of people standing on the road, blocking the only exit to the world beyond the Indian village.

His own people.

John took his foot off the gas, and instantly felt the cold steel gun against his head.

"Keep going, " the deep voice ordered.

He stepped carefully on the gas, weaving through the ruts, peering into the rain for an opening that would permit their escape without harming anyone. People scattered in every direction as the speeding car closed in, sliding through the mud, until John saw only one man, alone, in the middle of the roadway, his hair dripping like the gutters of a house, his face shining with rainwater in the glow of the headlights. And no matter whether he steered left or right, Dylan Reed was directly in front of the car, backpedaling, daring the driver to run him over, his hands extended as if he were steering the car from in front of it.

A shot rang out from the back seat. A tiny hole appeared in the windshield as Rosalie threw herself across the backseat on top of Lake, clawing his eyes, groping for the gun. They were twenty yards from Reed now, his feet planted, hands extended toward them, as if he were reaching out, drawing the car toward him, when they hit a large rut and bounced out of control, the steering wheel ripping itself out of John's grip. He stood up on the brake, and they skidded violently out of control; regaining the wheel, he battled the car to a wrenching halt just as the two left wheels slid over the edge of the earth.

The car listed as Rosalie and Lake fell against the left rear door, rocking it precariously on its chassis. The crowd let out a collective cry as Lake looked out the window and saw the faraway desert floor awaiting his fall, and in his momentary lapse of concentration, Rosalie knocked the gun out of his hand, out the window, down, down hundreds of feet into the gray rain. Reed and several others grabbed everything they could reach—door handles, window frames, and bumpers—as John scrambled across the front seat and out the open window. With the car tilted on its side, the rain pelted in on Lake and Rosalie, as he held her in a chokehold around her throat; his other hand produced the second gun from his belt, and he stared up with terrified eyes at his would-be rescuers.

"Get back!" he yelled crazily. "Get back!"

But Rosalie had a hand free, and she forced Lake's hand up toward the ceiling, where Reed, now so far inside the car that he was committed to its fate as well, grabbed her arm. He felt the others pulling him from behind, holding his feet, ready to drag their bodies up the six feet of nearly vertical seat; now, he struggled against the last-ditch strength of the federal agent, who had planted his feet against the door frame, still holding Rosalie, fighting for the gun.

With a yell, she elbowed Lake hard in the midsection and bit him on the arm. Lake lost his grip, and the force of the crowd holding Reed's feet kicked in, pulling first him, then her, through the car window as if propelled by a coiled spring. Together, they landed on three other men in a heap of bodies, safe on the beautiful muddy earth.

As the black metal weapon flew into the mud, a man with thinning brown hair bent over, picked it up, and appeared in the car window above the suspended man spread-eagled on the back seat, wide-eyed with terror.

"Give it up, Bob," said William Scanlon. "It's over."

Epilogue: Serenade

It was late in the spring, a beautiful, quiet afternoon when the sweet smells of green, still fragrant before the summer's heat arrives, filled the breeze. And it was quiet—quiet enough to hear the birds as they flew past the solitary figure leaning against the "Pavement Ends" sign, where the road turned to dirt for as far as could be seen.

The sun had moved noticeably since the last time he'd looked. Only one car had gone past, two Indian women with two children in the backseat, and that was a long time ago; but he had nowhere else to go, so he sat there, watching the birds, strumming the small guitar he'd found that morning in a pawn shop near the train station.

They had kept Bob Lake confined until federal marshals came from Phoenix. And Scanlon, who'd made it clear that Reed was still considered a fugitive, kept him and Rosalie separate.

"You can come now and make a statement," Scanlon said. "I promise you I will see you are treated fairly. And you'll only have to do this once. You can get on with your life. Or you can stay here and make us get a court order."

"I've nothing to say you don't already know," Rosalie told him. "And I have a daughter here." In the end, Scanlon and Reed drove off to an airport and flew to Washington. There, he was asked the same questions a hundred times but had not been able to help much, for he had never seen the crime for which he had been hunted. As for the smugglers, they had carefully kept him and Rosalie from seeing their faces, and he would not know them again even if he saw them. In the end, Scanlon had arranged for his release if, to prevent the bureau's embarrassment, he agreed to make no public statements.

"We have Lake," the agent told him. "We'll find out what we need to know from him." He handed Reed a large envelope with his belongings, from his arrest in Connecticut. There was only one object in the pouch, the small wooden matchbox that slid open at each end.

"Tell me, just for myself," Scanlon asked, "where were you the night Giles was killed?"

Reed ran his finger over the edge of the crude relic, wondering the same thing, taking a long time to answer.

"Probably nowhere you'd understand."

"Try me."

"I was fighting in the French and Indian War."

Scanlon shook his head and smiled resignedly. By the time the newspapers, the same ones that had splashed the Fool across page 1, had carried the page 6 story of the dismissal, he was gone. No one mentioned that the real case was that two federal agents were smuggling drugs on the side and one had killed the other.

For six months he lived in New York City, renting the front room of a three-room apartment in Greenwich Village from a musician working the local clubs. Reed worked as a sometime bartender and dishwasher in three different local music clubs and spent his free late-night hours listening to the guitar players and songwriters. And after a while, when he thought it was safe, he had gone to see Jim Quisto. He spent one night there, and the two old friends went for a drive.

"Jim," Reed said at last, "thank you for what you did. I'd still be in jail except for you."

"Hey, man, what are friends for?" Quisto beamed. "Did they ever ask about this place?" He nodded toward the new building being erected on the site of the old plant.

"No, nothing. What's this going to be?"

"Another plant. They say this time, they'll make it with the latest technology so it won't pollute. They say a lot of new standards they wouldn't apply to the old one will be used now."

Quisto sniffed the cool night air.

"Do you notice? I've gotten to like this place again. There's no smell."

Reed slapped his old buddy on the shoulder.

"Does it help?" he asked.

"A little. It won't bring any kids back. But I'll tell you one thing."

"What's that?"

"If this new one stinks, you'll get a call from me."

He'd stopped off in Chicago after that. He'd long since lost his apartment, and what remained of his belongings were at Lina's: two suitcases of old clothes, books, records, and papers. He wanted none of it.

"Thanks, Lina," he said. "Thank you for taking care of my stuff." He took it all out and threw it away, then went back to say goodbye. They stood in her doorway, a foot apart.

"So, back to the desert?"

"I guess so," he said. He wanted to say something to her, something wonderful they could treasure all their lives, a memory of their time together in case they were never to meet again. But in the wordless moment, they fell into each other's arms, standing there for some time in a last, long affectionate embrace.

"Goodbye, Rett," she whispered. "God bless you."

❧

The car stopped before he saw it, startling him as its shadow stretched out from the low western sun. He stood up and looked in the windshield. A young male with straight black hair and sunglasses on a well-bronzed face squinted back at him.

"Yo, dude!" the boy called out. "Can I play your guitar?"

He opened the door and slid onto the seat.

"Sure. If you like."

The driver grinned and stepped on the gas, and immediately they were bouncing along the dirt road, rippled like a giant washboard.

"Hey, man," the driver said. "Can you play 'Who'll Stop the Rain?'"

"No, not yet. Can you?"

"Sure. I'll show you when we get to town."

Reed nodded and stared out the window, as the long, flat plain stretched away to the high rocky cliffs in the distance. He had no idea what he would find there, but he had been drawn back to this place as surely as if he had always belonged there.

"When will that be?" he asked the young man.

The driver grinned again.

"Soon enough," he said.

⌘

The old woman clucked incessantly as she cradled the baby boy in her arms. With his fair skin and turquoise eyes, he was hardly what she was used to, but he was beautiful.

Glancing across the room, she saw Rosalie was awake.

"Your husband will be very proud."

"My husband?"

The old woman frowned.

"Where is your husband?"

But Rosalie turned her face to the wall, away from the gray-haired woman with her hair pulled tight behind her wise old face. And the midwife's saddened heart went out to her.

"Look," she said. "He has your eyes. So beautiful." She sat on the edge of the bed, placing the child in the mother's arms.

⌘

He waved goodbye and watched the taillights vanish around the next bend, into the gathering evening. There was still some red in the western sky, enough to see by; he slung the guitar and his small pack over his shoulder and began to walk into town, still humming the tune the boy had played for him in the picnic area.

The first thing he saw was the hulk of the brown station wagon, rusting and half sunk into the soft sand five hundred feet below.

"That's my car," John had protested. "It's government property."

"And who is the government," replied Michael Lanaka, "but the people?" And with the villagers' refusal to help, John, unable to hold it by himself, had watched as the car slid over the muddy cliff, to remain there below the town until it dissolved into the elements.

But now, the streets were deserted as Dylan Reed walked into town. He did not know where to go, so he pulled his jacket together and searched the narrow streets for something familiar. At last, he spied the small white house where he'd once slept, the anthropologist's house. He knocked on the door.

An old woman came out, her graying black hair pulled severely behind her head. She stood there with her arms folded and stared at him, quickly concealing a small gasp as she recognized the man standing before her.

"Hello," he began. "I'm looking for a woman named Rosalie. Can you help me?"

"Who wants to know?"

"My name is Dylan Reed."

The woman glanced quickly inside, then stepped outside and closed the door behind her.

"Why have you come here?"

"I told you," he said. "I'm looking for Rosalie Lenoir, a younger woman, about this tall, long red hair. Can you tell me where she is?"

She looked him over carefully. Finally, she reached out and tapped the guitar with her extended finger.

"You must sing," she said.

"Sing?"

"Sing," she repeated. Abruptly she turned and went back inside. He heard the door being locked behind her.

He knocked again, but this time no one came.

He stood before the house. Sing? Sing what? He paced around in the street, having no reason to stay but unable to go away. Again and again, he went back to the house, seeing only a glimmer of light shining from inside through the window frame. Was she near? Was she anywhere in this town?

He took the guitar off his shoulder and sat down on the ground, leaning his back against the cool wall of the house. Working the instrument into a harmonious tuning that rang sweet and clear even when he took his left hand completely off the strings, he plucked a chord and let his mind drift.

"It's a song that you've heard," he whispered to himself. That's it. Let the mind go on automatic, find its own song, he told himself, as he coaxed the notes from the guitar and began to sing.

> It's a song that you've heard
> It's a story been told before
> Still it feels like the first
> Come close, I will tell you more
> The way that it feels
> To be here standing on this shore
> With the wind at my back
> Calling you to your open door

The plaza was quiet. In several nearby houses, they listened with one ear as the women busied themselves cleaning up after dinner.

> The words are not grand
> They come from my open heart
> As I search for your love
> Many nights we have been apart
> The song is the way
> To whisper the dream you see
> Walk away, walk away
> Gypsy girl, walk away with me

The song came to a stop, but the guitar went on playing in his fingers. Still seated on the ground, he began again:

> It's a song that you've heard

The sky had darkened now. The stars were bright in the distance, and he had not seen anyone in the town since the old woman had gone inside.

It's a story been told before

A shooting star zoomed through the deep, dark blue above him, streaking the sky from afar.

Still it feels like the first

A whisper of wind brought some leaves circling through the plaza, swirling quietly in the otherwise still air.

Come close, I will tell you more

Across the plaza someone dropped a saucepan on its way to the shelf, letting it clank loudly to the floor.

The way that it feels

To the west, heat lightning flickered against the mountains like a million lightning bugs begging for attention.

To be here standing on this shore

A mosquito landed on his arm; he blew it off lightly, exhaling between the words of the song.

With the wind at my back

Two children peeked around the edge of a house; laughing, they ran away, unafraid that he'd seen them.

Calling you to your open door

There was a beam of light on the ground next to him, slanting out from the house.

The words are not grand

She was there, framed in the doorway by the smoky light, barefoot in a full-length white nightdress, her long red hair loose around her face. He stopped playing and stood up, his legs stiff from sitting so long. But he continued to sing.

They come from my open heart

He took her arm and drew her toward him, slowly stepping back onto the hard sand.

As I search for your love

He held her by the shoulders, turning her slowly to catch the faint evening light.

Many nights we have been apart

Around, around, they turned slowly, drawing nearer and nearer, as he held her eyes with his.

The song is the way

He drew her close, and she offered no resistance, gripping the sleeve of his shirt with her fingers.

To whisper the dream you see

She was in his arms now, turning slowly in the plaza, her face held up, looking into his eyes. A distant bird chirped in the darkness as the villagers waited behind their ageless walls. She reached up with her hand

and took the back of his head, sliding her fingers through his shaggy hair, drawing his face toward her.

"I knew you'd come back," she said, and she kissed him, long and sweet. With a soft smile, she looked in his eyes.

"Do you love me?"

"Yes," he said. "You know I do. And you?"

She leaned over and bit his ear playfully.

"Yes," she said. "And there's someone you should meet."

Printed in the United States
by Baker & Taylor Publisher Services